D0392205

What the Heart Knows

William W. Johnstone

What the
Heart Knows

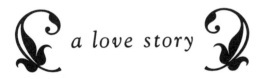 *a love story*

KENSINGTON BOOKS

KENSINGTON BOOKS are published by

Kensington Publishing Corp.
850 Third Avenue
New York, NY 10022

Library of Congress Card Catalog Number: 95-076007
ISBN 0-8217-5028-3

First Printing: August, 1995

Printed in the United States of America

I walked a mile with Pleasure
She chattered all the way,
But left me none the wiser
For all she had to say.
I walked a mile with Sorrow,
and ne'er a word said she;
But, oh, the things I learned from her,
When Sorrow walked along with me.

—Robert Browning Hamilton

What the
Heart Knows

 *After Cody*

I drank a lot after Cody. Came very close to stepping over that invisible mark that separates day-to-day reality from the hazy fog of booze. But that's all behind me now—at least most of the time.

One morning, with what had to be the worst hangover of my life pounding in my head, I looked at my memory of Cody in the clear light of day.

I relived each chapter and decided it was time to get on with my life before I drank myself to death or drowned in a pool of self-pity.

I fixed a cup of coffee and realized I could finally think about Cody without a hollow, sad sensation in the pit of my stomach. It was a good feeling.

Cody . . . ah, Cody.

She was like the wind; she was wild and cutting and could be profane; other times she was like a beautiful butterfly—drifting, soaring, graceful. She could be as a raging gale, those lovely eyes flashing, and then change into something soft and gentle, landing gently on the back of your hand. Her touch was velvet, and I loved her.

No. I *love* her. And part of me always will. I know, I know, sentimentality and all that. To admit to feelings, to step away from all that macho crap males are taught from childhood, to sit down and bawl and to hell with who sees you. Well, a man has to grow up. It just took me a little longer than most.

Cody was many things: tough and fragile and gentle and hateful and caring. She was no angel, and never pretended to be, although that's how I like to think of her. It's said that one only remembers the good times. I don't know who ever said that, but he sure never was a horse's-butt like I used to be, and he sure as hell never met Cody.

The girl had a very deep, sensitive side. She'd cry at the sight of puppy dogs and kittens lying dead by the side of the road. Old tumble-down houses got her all misty-eyed at the thought of the dreams that died within their crumbling walls. She was a romantic. Sad movies and sad books made her cry, but she didn't like others to see that. It took me a while to understand. When I did, it was too late.

Really, it was too late for us before we ever began. She could see that. I couldn't.

I finally understood that she covered up a lot of fear with smart-aleck remarks. She was afraid of her emotions and her self-esteem was very shaky. That's my opinion. You can judge for yourself.

Butterflies always make me think of Cody. Probably always will. I made the mistake of treating Cody like a butterfly. I thought she wanted just to sail on the wind, drifting effortlessly through life with no cares and worries. Just a beautiful sight, flying high.

I was wrong.

She was a free spirit, and she would have fit right in with the hippies of the "Sick Sixties." I am glad she wasn't old enough to have been a part of that torn time. But had she been, it would have been Her Thing, Man. She would have been all caught up in the marching and the demonstrations. And yet, Cody would have done those things because she really believed in them. I know that now.

As for me, I was too busy with college to pay much attention to war protesters. Besides, it was just about over when I graduated. And for reasons many people have yet to understand, after I got out of college I enlisted in the army, eventually becoming a part of a special operations unit and spending a good many months in Central America . . . among other places. Doing what is nobody's business but mine.

Cody never could understand why I wouldn't talk about those years in a spec op unit. She never understood why I couldn't talk about what I did.

I never think about that time in my life. Mostly I just think about Cody.

Sincere is a word that fits Cody, although there was a time when I doubted that. But that was a time when I was doubting many things. She was sincere and good, but I have to admit now that she also had a touch of the mercenary. Maybe all women do. And Cody could retreat to that tiny part of herself when things around her became too much. When the seas got too rough or the walls started closing in.

Anyway, that's my theory. And for all the love I felt for

her, it was always laced with sorrow. Cody did not have an easy life.

And I damn sure didn't make it any easier.

Don't misunderstand the tense in describing Cody. She's alive and well and happy, too, or so I'm told. God knows she deserves some happiness.

It's been a few years since I attempted, foolishly, to understand what the heart knows: you can't catch the wind. It's invisible quicksilver, an unseen game of the old pea under the shell; but in this game you don't gamble with money—you gamble with your heart.

Sometimes when I've fallen off my current two-drink wagon, I stand in the darkness of my backyard, listening to the wind sing and sigh, and put out my hand to the breeze for a few seconds. That is when it all comes crashing back, velvet soft and deeply painful. The touch, the scent, the softness. The hello and goodbye.

And I'm lost momentarily, but not in self-pity. Not now. Not anymore. Now I can savor the good times, the loving and the laughter.

Cody used to laugh at me when I'd turn sour and start bitching about people her age. You see, we were a full generation apart, but we were so much in love we thought we could bridge that chasm. At least I did. Maybe she did, too. And maybe, given a bit more time, we could have. I'll never know.

As for me, I think often of the first time and the last time I saw Cody. Pleasure and Sorrow.

And butterflies? Well, if you must touch a butterfly, let it touch you, enjoy the sensation, and let it go. For if you handle a butterfly too roughly, it can no longer fly.

 One

I didn't like the man. Not from the first meeting in New York City, when he'd flown up to interview me. I've learned to trust the invisible needle on my indicator, and the vibes I got from Vic Goodman were red-lining the over-modulation mark.

He was one of those big-bellied, lard-butted success stories, complete with a joke for every occasion, big salesman's smile, firm handshake, and little cold, piggy eyes. But he was to be my new boss, and as national sales manager of his company, this promotion meant my salary jumped astronomically. In addition to a percentage of profits, a car, house, and all the other perks that went with top-level personnel, I would be just one jump from the top.

I guessed I could put up with the loudmouth for that kind of security.

Besides, I would be returning to the South. I had been too many years away from magnolias and the lovely ladies of Dixie. Not that the South has a monopoly on lovely ladies;

New York City is full of beautiful women. But there is something about southern women that I had missed over the years. I think it's the bitch in them.

Vic had sent a limo to pick me up at Hartsfield Atlanta International.

"Lawrence J. Baldwin," Vic Goodman gushed, shaking my hand. I resisted an impulse to wipe my palm on my trousers while wondering if I was about to make the biggest mistake of my career. "Good to have you with us, boy. Yes, sir, it shore is. I think you'll find us a good deal easier to get along with down here—back home, I should say. You been up north with the damn yankees just too long, boy. 'Way too long." He chuckled and winked.

I smiled and nodded in agreement.

"Yes, sir," Vic repeated. "You been away for a long time, son. How many years, Lawrence-boy? Twelve, fifteen? Yeah, at least. Too long for a southern boy." He waved at a sofa in the lavishly appointed office. "Sit, sit. You musta forgot, boy: we're laid back and easy down here."

I sat. "I haven't been away that long, Mr. Goodman."

"Aw, hell, son! Call me Vic. My daddy were Mr. Goodman."

"Right, Vic. And it's Larry, not Lawrence."

"Gotcha. Vic and Larry it is. Kind of early in the day for a drink . . . but what the hell! Back in my navy days, we used to have a skipper who would say a man hadn't ought to take a drink 'less the sun was over the yardarm.' Then he'd wink and say, 'But the sun's always over the yardarm somewheres!' "

I dutifully laughed at the old joke and knew that while Vic

was pouring the bourbon he was studying me closely in the mirror behind the wet bar.

Just a touch of gray at the temples. Thick, carefully trimmed dark brown hair, worn shorter than present style dictates. My weight has remained fairly constant over my forty years, time treating me much more kindly than I deserved, considering the lifestyle. One-eighty-five spread over six feet, two inches. Still lean-waisted with a lot of meat in chest, shoulders, and arms. Big hands, thick wrists, the knuckles faintly scarred from a number of brawls back in my younger days. Various ladies have said, from time to time, that my looks are more rugged than handsome. Dark eyes that never give away too much.

"Soda or water, Larry?"

"Water, please. Don't drown it."

He placed the drinks on a low table and took a seat beside me on the leather couch that stretched from wall to wall. Vic owned the largest office supply company in North America. Among other things.

"It's nice havin' you here, Larry. But a surprise. You 'bout a month early."

"I wanted to get to work. Spend some time covering the territory—as much of it as possible—and getting to know my people and some of the bigger accounts in the Southeast. I think work is what I need right now, Vic. The best thing for me."

"Sure, boy. Sure it is." Vic patted me on the knee with a big, fat hand, a huge diamond ring on his pinkie. I do not like men patting me. "I understand, son. I purely do. I was right sorry to hear 'bout you and your little woman bustin' up. Damn shame, I said."

Little woman? My ex would have smacked him in the mouth had she been present. I noticed Vic's Georgia corn-pone accent came and went, and I wished he would take it and stuff it. He was a self-made man, yes, but he also held a degree and knew how to use proper English. But I understood. A good salesman is like a chameleon: you deal with rednecks, you speak their language.

"It was for the best, Vic. We'd been living apart for some time. The marriage just fell apart. Luckily, there were no children."

I was not going to volunteer more. Vic would have to drag it out of me, and I felt he would surely try. He was on a blood-hound trail, and besides, he was a nosy bastard.

"Divorce final, Larry?"

"Oh, yeah. It was a quickie." Come on, you old fart. Move on to something else.

But he wasn't ready. "She must have been one of them career women, huh?" He made that sound nasty. "I've got a bunch of 'em workin' for me. Damn government and their affirmative action. Well," he sighed, "I don't like them bossy women types very much, but they do their part. A few of 'em handle some big accounts. They keep the purchasin' agents happy by spreadin' their legs, I reckon."

Knowing he was expecting it, I smiled and nodded. Dance with the devil, Larry; keep the boss happy.

His face lit up like a neon sign. "Me and you gonna get along fine, Larry-boy. We think alike." He chuckled. "I think women have a place in business an' all that, but it damn shore ain't tellin' no man what to do. You know how we feel about that down here in the South."

But all that's changing, Vic, I wanted to say. But didn't. I still smiled, knowing full well he would misinterpret it. I had missed most aspects of the South, but not good ol' boys like Vic Goodman.

"Well, Larry, let's get back to you. Boy, when you played for Georgia, them was the days, huh? Hey—Hey—Hey!" He slapped me on the leg and I resisted an impulse to break all the fingers on that hand. "Love that game of football!" Vic shouted.

I really thought for a moment he was going to jump up and start cheering. But he calmed down and contented himself with recounting all the great plays of my college career. He didn't know and I wasn't about to tell him that I had not watched an entire game of football in years.

"Then damned if you didn't turn down all them pro offers and join the army. Never did understand that, Larry-boy. Boggled my mind, it did. You could have been one of the greatest runnin' backs ever to come out of Georgia." He looked at me. "Why did you join up?"

My drink was too strong, but I sipped at it carefully, hoping the ice would soon melt and water it down. I hid my grimace before it could form on my face. I was weary of telling the story and wondered how many times I had told it. I also wondered why some people never manage to grow up. I didn't know that I had quite a way to go myself.

"Because I wanted to, Vic." He raised his shaggy eyebrows at that. I wondered why he didn't have the barber trim the damn things. "But that's only a part of it. I was confused by all the money being tossed at me. I was tired of the game, and quite frankly, I believed then and now that I wouldn't have lasted in the pros."

"Well, I'll be damned," Vic said after a moment. "Well, hell, I was in the navy. I can understand your wantin' to serve your country. We both from the South." He looked at me for a moment. "You wore one of them green berets, didn't you?"

"Yeah, I did."

"Word got back here that you was doin' work for the CIA, too."

I said nothing.

"I understand that you can't talk about it."

Then I caught his expression and knew what Vic was thinking: all those stories that surround special operations people. Green Berets, Marine Force Recon, Rangers, SEALs, Air Force Combat Controllers. I suppressed a sigh.

Yes, Virginia, there is a Santa Claus. No, Virginia, spec ops people are not invincible. We bleed, we die, we have all the human emotions: we hate, cry, laugh, love. Well . . . most of us love. I had yet to really experience that.

I met Vic's eyes and knew what was coming next. I was not disappointed.

"You boys really get all that trainin', Larry? All that killin' stuff—hand-to-hand combat kind of thing?"

"Quite a bit of it, Vic."

He looked at his drink on the coffee table. Here again, I knew what was coming, and as before, I was not disappointed. "You ever kill a man, Larry?"

Memories flung me back over the years. Sweaty, bloody memories. I nodded my head, not trusting my voice.

"With your hands, Larry?" he asked, his voice no more than a whisper.

"Yes, Vic." I hoped the conversation could end now, or at least turn to a less gruesome topic. "With my hands."

"Ever use a knife on anyone, Larry?"

He just wouldn't let go. I looked at him. I guess he found the answer in my eyes.

"Damn!" Vic said.

And on that happy note, I said I'd better check into a motel and see about opening the house. I told Vic I'd see him first thing in the morning and start getting squared away in my office.

"You behave yourself tonight, now, you hear?" He winked at me. "This here town is just full of good-lookin' women just waitin' for a handsome stud like you."

"I'll be careful."

As I closed the door to his office, I noticed Vic still sitting on the couch, a serious expression on his face. He was looking at his hands, perhaps wondering how it would feel to kill a man with them.

I'm sure it affects men differently, but one thing is certain: you never forget it.

"Reason I moved out here to Pine Hills, Larry," Vic said, while giving me the personal guided tour of the town, "was to get away from them damn niggers. Atlanta's full of 'em and gettin' fuller. Oh, I employ a whole bunch in the factory. Got to, the damn government makes you. I even got some Jews workin' for me. Why, Larry-boy . . ."

I tuned him out, letting him ramble and spew his hate. I

had to turn my head to hide a sudden grin. My ex-wife was Jewish. I'm no psalm-singing, hanky-stomping liberal, but neither am I a racist. That and homosexuality are about the only two things I've never been accused of.

But I didn't want to discuss race relations with Vic. People like Vic are going to have to die out, taking all their fears and hates and blind prejudices with them. But even that won't solve it, 'cause people like Vic pass their views along to their kids.

"But on the other hand, Larry," Vic was saying as I tuned him back in, "I got me a fine-lookin' high yeller gal over in Atlanta. I keep her in clothes and a nice apartment and spendin' money. I see her ever' now and then." He grinned and pulled at his crotch. "Talkin' 'bout her gets me all worked up. I just might have to take a run over there later on this afternoon. Know what I mean, Larry-boy?"

I gazed out the window, seeing my reflection staring back at me. Suddenly I didn't like what I saw, and that startled me, for I've always been out for number one and to hell with anyone else.

"Yeah, Vic. I know what you mean."

Liar. Hypocrite. Go back and read that line from Tennessee Williams again, the one about hypocrisy and mendacity. Fits you to a T. You talk out of both sides of your mouth, just like you did in New York. You're still a horse's ass, Baldwin.

"Tell me about that Spanish stuff, Larry. Was it any good? I ain't never had me none of that."

I knew what to say and I said it. "I never had no bad, Vic. You?"

He howled and slapped the steering wheel at the old joke.

"Whoooee, no, boy. Wors' I ever had was pure-dee wonder-ful."

Pine Hills, Georgia, is a pretty town, about thirty miles outside of Atlanta. And as is usual with southern towns, it was full of good-looking women of all ages. If the South ever does rise again, it will be due in no small part to its women, not because of a bunch of tobacco-chewin', snuff-dippin', crotch-scratchin', coon-huntin', honky-tonkin' good ol' boys.

I noticed a gaggle of girls getting in a convertible. We had stopped at a traffic light, so I had ample time to admire their charms, which were considerable. They were in their late teens, certainly no more than twenty, and lovely to look at. But while twenty-year-old females were nice to watch, I had only involved myself with one woman with that much of an age spread on me. We didn't have anything to talk about. And when she did talk, I didn't know what in the hell she was talking about.

Vic caught the direction of my eyes and smiled.

"Ain't they something, Larry-boy? Lord have mercy on ol' boys like us, huh? Them is prime. Shame we ain't young. We'd be humpin' ourselves into the grave. That blond-headed one, that's the mayor's daughter. One beside her is Toni White. The twins is Judy and Jenny Davenport. They're all good girls, if you know what I mean. Selective about who they give it to. But that slut over there," he pointed as his voice hardened, "comin' out of the dress shop—the one with two P's—shop-pay, I guess you'd call it . . ."

I looked at him to see if he was putting me on. He looked serious.

". . . That there is one bad little gal. I know that for a pure-dee fact. She's poison."

I looked. Then looked again. I saw a petite young woman, very shapely, maybe five-three. Shining black hair, worn long, hanging down her back. Somehow I knew her eyes were blue, but a very pale blue. I don't know how I knew. She was very, very pretty. I had to smile at the way she was dressed. She was a rainbow in a small conservative Georgia town, letting people know she dressed the way that pleased her, and if they didn't like it, they could damn well lump it. Jeans and high-heeled boots and a bright red shirt and a sash for a belt. I had to smile. I admired her spunk.

She caught me looking at her as Vic drove on. She tossed her head, just a touch of arrogance in her stride. I liked her style.

"What's wrong with her, Vic?" We drove past as the girl marched along, head held high.

"Oh, hell, Larry. You name it. Smokes that old dope. Takes pills. Probably uses cocaine, too. Drinks to ex-cess and cusses like a drunken dock worker. Did you get a good look at that slut? A-sashayin' down the street, just a-swingin' and a-shakin' her ass? Umm-umm-umm." He shook his head. "Bad little ol' gal, that one is. Damn shame, too."

"Oh?" She looked like a class act to me.

"Oh, yeah. It's a shame, all right. Her mama and daddy was such good folks. Fine people, the both of them. Good, decent, hard-workin' folk. Church-goin' folk, just like you and me, boy. Just common folk. They was killed four, five years ago. Since they passed, that little girl has run plumb hog-wild. Lord, Lord, the stories folk tell on that child."

Child? "She's in high school?"

"Oh, no. She's 'bout twenty, twenty-one, I reckon. Lots of folks 'round here would like to see her leave town. She's a bad influence on the other children in town. I don't know what she's doin' still hangin' 'round Pine Hills. Maybe she's sellin' that butt of hers. I just don't know. I put a bug in Chief Pardue's ear to keep an eye on her. He'll roust her if he ever gets the chance. She's got a little bitty income from insurance her folks had. Three or four hundred dollars a month. Don't work half the time. Lives with an old auntie who is half nuts. Poor old woman don't know what time of day it is, much less where that naughty little niece of hers is gone and up to all hours of the night. Damn shame, I say."

I got the impression that Vic knew a hell of a lot about this girl, and there was more to the story. And, if I were a betting man, which I'm not, I'd bet that Vic would just love to bed down with the kid. I held that thought and listened to him rattle on.

"Yes, sirree, boy. Got one in every town, I reckon. And that back yonder is Pine Hills' female-type hippie person. Dresses like a damn gypsy. Them jeans so tight don't leave nothin' to the mind. Pitiful. No tellin' how much of that stuff she's spread around."

Vic finally ran out of bad things to say about the girl and we headed back to the plant complex, located just on the outskirts of town. Moving the plant out of the city and into the sticks, so to speak, had been a very wise move on Vic's part. As I would later learn, it gave the customers a relaxed, homey atmosphere in which to have very subtle business pressure applied to them. And the motel, a nice one, with excellent food and a well-stocked and serviced private bar with sexy wait-resses, was located just a few minutes from the main show-room and plant complex.

The Pine Hills Inn. Complete with whores.

Vic owned the motel. And the whores.

"That kid back in town, Vic. The one you talked about?"

"What kid, Larry? Oh! Well, don't you fret none 'bout her, Larry-boy. It's like I said: ever' town's got one, and Little Cody is all ours."

"Cody?"

"That's her name. Cody West."

I threw myself into work with everything I had in me and the summer drifted lazily along. It was not uncommon for me to be at work, in my office, at seven in the morning and stay until long after dark, Saturdays included. I'm not a social ani-mal and never have been. Parties, if I attend them at all, are purely business for me. I know sales, know people, know my product, know stats, and can read a demographic the way oth-ers pore through a fine novel, seeing things that another per-son could not.

In just under four months, with perhaps half that time spent in the air and on the road, I brought our sales—nation-wide—up several percentage points. Vic was beside himself with joy.

"I ain't never seen nothin' like it in all my borned days, Larry," he said. I had been summoned to his office for lunch. Kansas City steaks, rare, baked potato dripping with country butter and sour cream, sourdough bread he had flown in from San Francisco, and green salad. Iced tea. "You made yourself a nice chunk of change, too, boy." He smiled. " 'Fess up, now, Larry: any truth to the rumor floatin' around the office 'bout you screwin' that good-lookin' sales rep of ours up in Knoxville?"

I had been warned that nothing escaped Vic's attention—he had spies located all over the country. "Marjorie?" I shrugged. "Yes. And now that I've learned she has a big mouth, she can pack it in and get out."

Vic put down his fork and chewed his steak in silence for a few seconds, his eyes on my face. "Huh! I guess the talk is true about you, Larry. You're a hard man. Marjorie, now, she's a good salesman."

Vic Goodman wouldn't say *salesperson* under threat of death.

"Yes, she is. I certainly agree. She won't have any problem finding a job. I'll give her a good recommendation. But she can't be trusted. This proves it."

"You want loyalty, eh, Larry? Total loyalty. But to you, or to me?"

"I'm loyal to you, Vic: the sales force is loyal to me. I carry out your orders. You and I, Vic, one and the same. That's the way I see it."

He slowly nodded his big head. "All right. It's your ball game. You're calling the signals. You can fire her if you want to. But, Larry, she's liable to kick up one unholy fuss about this."

"Screw her."

"I thought you did!" Vic howled with laughter, little bits of steak and salad spraying the table. And me. I pretended not to notice.

Tactful Larry Baldwin, that's me. Larry-boy with the very sharp little knife in his hands, ready to stick it into anyone who gets in his way on the climb up to the top of the corporate ladder. That's the name of the game.

Besides, I hadn't screwed Marjorie. We didn't have the time. She just didn't want to admit the truth, so she made up a lie.

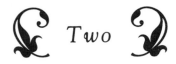

Two

I dutifully attended the first few football games of the season with Vic. Naturally, he had the best seats money could buy. Georgia was his alma mater and he was a heavy contributor to the athletic fund. And that was the only program he contributed to. Vic didn't give a damn if the kids learned anything in the classrooms. Just win games. He hollered and squalled and got half-drunk as he urged the 'Dawgs on to victory. Had me introduced as a former All-American running back and ex-Special Forces.

It was embarrassing.

After the first few games, along about the first of October, I began having to go out of town on business, leaving early on a Friday. At first, Vic was unhappy about that, but as the sales picture continued its upward spiral, he got over his disappointment and left me alone about missing the Big Game.

But he never did understand why the game no longer held any interest for me. I had played in high school for several reasons: in a football town, the players get better treatment from the teachers and the townspeople, the best players get the best-looking women, and it was my ticket to college. In college, I got the same treatment, plus money under the table from fans with more money than sense. And I also got a lot of women under the sheets.

But when I got out of the army, I found something that I enjoyed more than sports: the tough world of business; the climb to the top; the fierceness of that game; the nasty world of success, stepping on anyone who got in my way. I became known as a man who could get it done and the hell with how.

I have never had any patience with softness in people in the business world. It's a dog-eat-dog life and watch your back and your flanks. I had learned the fine art of brutal guerrilla warfare as a member of a spec ops team, and brought that knowledge with me into my civilian career.

At age forty, I was a stepper, going places: don't get in Baldwin's way, 'cause he'll damn sure walk right over you.

But I had paid my dues, and they had been expensive.

The climb up had taken all my time, eight days a week and seven nights. But I did it. Yeah, I lost a wife along the way, made a lot of enemies, had never found love—didn't understand it, didn't have time for it. Now I was in the big money, and don't let a base salary fool you. A base is just what it implies: a base from which to work. It does not take in the percentages from overall sales; the kickbacks; the luxury car I don't pay for; the credit cards; the beautiful home that comes with the position; and more. Much more.

Power.

But there is one thing that is very true: if you do make it to the top the way I did, it's lonely. You have few friends and you really can't trust anyone. But it's worth it. Vic was only in his mid-to-late fifties, but he was already talking retirement and I knew I was being groomed to take over when he stepped down.

And I was both feared and respected. I could sense that after Marjorie was canned. Larry Baldwin is a bastard, a one hundred percent SOB. Just do your job to the best of your ability and you'll be well paid. Screw up, and you'll be gone.

Maybe I was more of a bastard than I should have been. But I never asked anyone to do a job that I couldn't or wouldn't do myself. I started at damn near the bottom in this business, so I knew I could do it all. Even today I'm hard to work for. Demanding. But I pay well, listen to suggestions all up and down the line, and compensate the good ones.

You just can't be a one hundred percent nice guy and run any large company. You've got to be part son of a bitch. That's just the way it is.

Marjorie would still be working for the Goodman Company if she'd just kept her damned mouth shut.

So maybe I am a hard-ass. But up to that juncture in my life, I sure as hell hadn't lost any sleep over it.

But that was before I met Cody.

Autumn slipped almost unnoticed into the coolness of late fall, then fall quietly stretched her arms to embrace the first cold wave of the season. The local radio stations began programming a few Christmas tunes and the shopping malls geared up for Santa Claus and the bottom line: profit.

The first week of December, Vic informed me that he was taking his wife and heading for the south of France. For years, he'd been spending winters first in France, then in the Caribbean. But he'd missed the last two years because he didn't have anyone back at the office he could trust to run things. Now he had me. *So you take care now, you hear, Larry-boy, and I'll see you in a couple of months.*

This was the first time I had been inside the Goodman mansion, for as Vic had said, "I don't never have none of my people out to my house, Larry-boy. You the first ever. But I'm thinkin' hard on you someday headin' up this company of mine. CEO sound good to you? I thought it would. My boy don't want nothin' to do with it, and I ain't gonna push him.

"No, sir, Larry-boy, I lead my life, my people lead theirs. Good policy to maintain. We be big buddies at the office, on the course, in the bars. But home life is somethin' else."

That suited me just fine, for I had heard office talk that Vic's pride and joy, Mike Goodman, was a royal pain in the ass and a spoiled brat. I had no desire to meet him. Vic's other kids, all older, were married and gone. I thought it odd that none of them wanted anything to do with their daddy's business. But Vic never spoke of them and I never brought up the subject.

Vic was anxious to get going so I saw them off at the airport. I would just bet that Vic, with his on-again, off-again corn pone vernacular was a real hit in France. Especially since he referred to the French as "Frogs."

I headed into the city where I had a pre-arranged room at a nice hotel. I planned to drift in and out of a few bars, then have an early dinner and sleep late in the morning. With the AIDS situation the way it was, I was very careful about sex.

There were plenty of available women in Pine Hills, but

nearly all the ones I'd met were married. If I have a moral streak concerning bed-partners, that's it. No married women. That, I suppose, goes back to my parents. My mother would screw anything that wore pants, and my father was an alcoholic who died in his mid-fifties. My mother was in her mid-forties when she followed him. Shot right between the eyes by a jealous wife.

It was one of the best and most expensive hotels in the city and the bell captain and I knew each other without ever having been introduced. That is to say, I knew he could get what I wanted, for a price—and what I wanted was information.

It was a short five minutes before he knocked on my door. He knew my clothes and luggage suggested money and the eye contact down in the lobby told him I wanted to see him.

"Where's the action in this town?"

He shrugged. "How do you like them?"

"I like them with a pussy."

He mentioned a few bars and then stood there, smiling.

"Drop the other shoe."

His smile broadened and he held out one hand. I put a bill in it, he gave me a name. "That's where a lot of available stuff hangs out. They're class broads. Most of them executive types, some in their twenties. They all like a good time. Drinks, dinner, then maybe sack time if you hit it off. And they're careful, if you know what I mean. Wedding rings come off before you enter the place. People go there to have fun. If you can talk and don't get too kinky, you'll do all right."

It was a damn rock and roll club, the kind with a mouthy

deejay spinning records and doing his best to be cute. My rock and roll years were well behind me—I lean toward classical music—but I figured my head could stand the noise for a drink or two while I looked over the crowd.

"Crown Royal and water," I shouted in an attempt to make myself heard over the wailing. I couldn't understand the lyrics. I wasn't all that sure I wanted to.

I couldn't tell if it was male, female, or a group. Whoever it was sounded as if he, she, they, or it was in excruciating pain. I think it's called Heavy Metal.

If a society is judged by its music, we're in serious trouble. Then I grinned, thinking: Come on, Baldwin. You're just getting old, that's all. Most of these young people will outgrow this noise and you know it. You did. So relax.

The song ended to a burst of applause. I resisted an impulse to join in—my applause would have been for an entirely different reason: the song was over and my hearing was returning. Slowly.

Then the deejay came on with his patter and that was as bad as the music. Whatever happened to announcers who knew how to speak English?

My distaste must have been very evident, for a female voice said, "If you don't like the music, why don't you just leave?"

I started to make some smart-assed reply, but as I turned my head, the sight of midnight-black hair and pale blue eyes stilled my tongue.

It was the girl Vic had pointed out. Cody West.

"I didn't know what kind of place this was until I got in here," I replied. "Be a shame to waste a good drink by getting up and leaving. And aren't you a little young to be in a bar?" I really didn't know what the legal drinking age was in this state. But if she wanted to get cute-mouthed, so could I.

That arrogant toss of the head I remembered seeing on the street. "That's none of your business, now, is it? Besides, I'm twenty-two."

I gave her my best smile. "Would that I were."

She did not return the smile. "Yeah, I bet. I can see you're really getting on."

My reply was as dry as I could make it. "Thanks. I certainly appreciate that."

She hissed at me. Honest-to-God *hissed* at me. Like a damn lizard.

"What do you do for an encore? Bite? Have you had all your shots?"

"I don't think I like you very much," she said. "As a matter of fact, I know I don't like you very much."

"You're breaking my heart."

"Yeah? I can see you're all torn up. Big deal!"

I could understand why this young lady just might irritate the hell out of a lot of people. "I think I'll tell the bartender your ID is a fake, kid. How's that grab you?"

Ice touched the pale blue, freezing the fiords in her eyes. They were the most beautiful I'd ever seen. I wondered just how old she really was.

"That would be a real crappy thing to do, mister," she spat at me. "But I guess you big-shot executive types get your kicks by . . ."

"Whoa!" I held up a hand in a gesture of peace before she could get wound up. "Hold it right there. I was only joking."

"Your whole generation is a joke," she popped right back. "Your humor is very unfunny. It's sick." She lifted her glass. "Here's a toast to the generation that gave us those wonderful days of Vietnam."

I almost got up and walked out, right then. I wish I had. In a way.

"I wasn't in Vietnam. And whether you believe it or not, there are some of us who felt it was a just cause."

"I'm not one of them."

"I never would have guessed. Besides, you weren't even *born* when the damn war *ended*. Look, we're getting off to a really rotten start. Let me introduce myself and we'll start over. I'm . . ."

"I know who you are," she cut me off. "Pine Hills is a small town, remember? Larry J. Baldwin. Big-shot executive with the Goodman Company. Probably being groomed to take over when lard-ass Goodman retires, or dies, preferably the latter. You make a lot of money ordering people around like slaves. Big military hero-type somewhere. How many little babies did you kill while trying to save the natives from their own relatives? You were a hot-shot college jock. You live in a fancy house with a swimming pool. Heated, no doubt. There's more, but I find the rest of it just as boring and depressing. And I'm sure that probably sums you up."

I sat on the stool and stared at her, my drink forgotten. For some reason, the girl fascinated me. And irritated me. "You're an opinionated bitch, aren't you?"

She made a terrible face at me and I had to laugh.

"All right. Then I'm flattered and very impressed with your

knowledge of my background . . . however off base it might be."

She centered those eyes square on mine. "There is nothing about you that impresses me. You work for Victor Goodman, who hates me and says vile, ugly things about me. And those things are not true. So if you work for him, you're probably like him in many ways, and if that's true, I *damn* sure don't have any use for you."

Again, I had to smile. Since I don't remember being young, and by that I mean it was hardscrabble around my home, with everybody working, I have a difficult time relating to today's young. This girl was so serious and damned beautiful at the same time. But . . . something about her brought a hard and swift pang of sorrow racing through me. Sorrow for her, not for me. I wondered briefly about that.

"Why does Vic hate you so, Cody?"

The eyes widened in surprise. "You know my name."

"Yes, I do. But that doesn't answer my question, does it?"

"I'm curious as to how—and why—you know my name. What have you been doing, following me around, skulking behind trees and peeking in my bedroom window? Are you some kind of pervert?"

She was good, but she just couldn't quite bring it off. The humor began twinkling in her eyes.

I got it then: she was having a good time putting me on.

"Very good, Cody. You're quite an actress."

She smiled. Lovely. "Had you going for a time, didn't I?"

"Yes, you sure did." My eyes drifted to a small pin on her shirt. Blouse. Whatever. A butterfly. "I know your name because Vic told me the first day I saw you, coming out of a dress shop."

She nodded. "I remember. Okay. Vic's son, Mike—he's about my age." She paused. "Are you going to go tell lard-ass everything I say?"

I laughed at the abrupt change. "No, Cody. I'm not going to do that."

"You promise?" she asked, almost childlike.

"I promise," I said solemnly. "You want me to spit and swear I'll get warts if I tell?"

She grinned at that. "I don't think the management would appreciate you spitting in here. Okay. Mike's a year older than me. He used to ask me out, over and over and over. He was a senior in high school, I was a junior. So . . . I went out with him. Big mistake. I went out with him one time. One time." Her voice was bitter. "The guy had hands like an octopus. Two octopuses. Octopi. I swear to God, he was all over me."

The music—if that's what it could be called—cranked up again, the deejay screaming insanely. He sounded like he was sitting on his balls and couldn't get off. Cody read the expression on my face and burst out laughing. She leaned close to me and I caught the scent of her. God help me, after all this time, after all I put her through, I have never been able to get that scent out of my head. And I have tried.

"It *is* too loud, Larry," she said, her lips close to my ear.

Well, now. First-name basis right off. And suddenly I wanted to bed her down. That surprised me, for I didn't strike up the conversation with that in mind. But now I had heady visions of getting the pants off of her.

I have never been so badly mistaken in all my years of chasing women.

"I'll buy you a cup of coffee and you can finish your story. How about it?"

I practically had to scream the words over the deafening music and several young men—the place was full of the under-twenty-five set—turned to look at me, disapproval stark in their eyes. Unspoken messages loud: Old rooster trying to hustle the young chick. Go pick on someone your own age, Dads. Like maybe in an old folks' home.

I met the hard and disapproving look of a young man in his early-to-mid-twenties. I wanted him to say something. He started to get off the bar stool and I smiled, about like a mongoose smiles at a cobra. The young wanna-be-bad suddenly had a change of heart. He didn't like the look in my eyes. He planted his butt back on the cushion of the stool, dropped his gaze, and began studying his drink. Maybe he had already found out the hard way that us old dudes don't fight fair.

I relaxed and turned my eyes back to Cody and found her studying me closely. She cocked her head, black silk falling over one pale blue eye. She smiled. "You wanted that boy to say something, didn't you, Larry?"

"He's not a boy, Cody. And yeah, it wouldn't have disappointed me if he had."

"I see. Well. Tell me, what comes after the coffee, Mr. Baldwin?"

Damn. *Mister*. Formal again. "Nothing," I lied. And lying is something a good salesman had better be able to do, and do superbly. "Want me to cross my heart?" I smiled at her.

That smile again. A slow pull of the lips in that beautiful

face. "You're lying," she whispered the words. I could only read her lips over a sudden burst of music.

The situation was wild. I don't do things like this. I'm calculating, manipulative; I plan things carefully. But I had never wanted to kiss a woman that badly in all my life.

"All right, Cody," I said, leaning close and speaking directly into her ear. "If that's what you believe." Her midnight hair smelled delicious and my fingers tingled to touch the raven softness of it. "So put me on an honor system. If I do or say something that offends you, tell me to back off or bug out. Deal?"

I realized that I had met one of those rare individuals it is almost impossible to lie to. This was going to be fun. A real challenge. But I would have to be very careful.

She nodded her head, brushing back her hair. "Okay. It's a deal, Dads." She laughed and stood up. "I had two drinks. Pay the bill, Pops."

 Three

The cold night air felt wonderful. I took a couple of deep breaths and said we'd walk until we found a cafe. Cody looked at me as if I had lost my mind.

"It's not safe to walk in this part of the city at night, Mr. Baldwin. I mean, I may hitch up here, but I don't walk in Atlanta at night."

"My name is Larry."

"*Mr. Baldwin* for now. Maybe *Larry* later. Okay?"

My turn to chuckle. I was beginning to like this young lady. "Okay—deal. And what in the hell do you mean, *you hitch up here?*"

"Hitchhike," she said, as if everybody did it and why was I making such a fuss?

"Are you nuts, Cody? That's dangerous. Why don't you drive or take a bus?"

"Lots of reasons. One, I don't have a car. Two, the bus schedule sucks. Three, thanks to Vic and Mike Goodman poisoning the entire town of Pine Hills against me, I have few friends left. Four, a lot of time I don't have the money. And in case you're wondering—and you are, I can tell—no, I'm not a hustler. Any girl who looks like anything at all rarely has to buy a drink back there." She jerked a thumb toward the rock joint. "But I was getting desperate tonight, I'll admit that."

I just couldn't believe what she was saying. "Don't you have any money, Cody?"

"No."

"Well . . . good God! Where do you sleep when you're in the city?"

"Usually I just crash in the bus station."

That brought me up short. I stopped her and stared down at her, disbelief in my eyes.

She smiled, and then laughed. "Oh, Larry. I'm just kidding you. I've got a room at the Y and I ride the bus home. I just wanted to see if you'd believe me."

Back on a first-name basis. "Well, I did believe you. Are you lying to me, Cody? Do you have any money at all?"

She dug in her purse and showed me a bus ticket, then opened her wallet—both purse and wallet were far from being new, I noticed—and showed me a few bills. She had some money, but damn little. She held up some one-dollar bills secured by a large paper clip.

"Taxi fare," she said with a smile. "I know exactly how much it is back to the Y from here."

I suddenly felt sorry for this little raven-haired rainbow, and at that moment, my feelings had nothing to do with sex. She picked up on my mood-shift very quickly. She was quick in the intuitive department.

"There's a funny look in your eyes, Larry. And your face has changed, too, kind of."

Perceptive, too. "Oh?" I shrugged it off. "Relief, maybe. I'm glad to be out of that damn joint. Glad to know you were only putting me on about sleeping in the bus station, that's all. Besides, the young studs back there didn't much like you leaving with me."

She had nothing to say to that. She looked at me, and I sensed she didn't buy my story. But she didn't argue. Finally she said, "Sure. Okay."

I took her arm—that's something we old folks do—and she seemed to like that. We started to walk. She said, "I am telling you, Larry: It—is—not—safe—to—walk—in—this— part—of—the—city—after—dark." She carefully enunciated each word, as one might speak to a child.

And looking back, maybe she *was* speaking to a child. I'd been the boss dog of the junkyard for years—all my life, really.

Arrogant? Yes, I was. Very much so. But no longer. Cody knocked that out of me.

I took her arm and began walking. "Cody, I've lived in cities for years. The last several years in New York City, and I think the Big Apple invented mugging. Last year two punks tried to mug me. I put both of them in the hospital." I was not bragging. Just stating hard facts.

She looked up at me. "What did the police have to say about that?"

"Are you kidding? Why involve them? If I'd done that, the bleeding hearts and sob sisters would've given the punks a medal and put me in jail."

She laughed. "Now I have something to hang over your head," she said with a smile in the neon night. A nice smile. Some little twist of emotion turned in me. It was sort of a gentle squeeze around the heart. I pushed it away, not knowing or caring what it meant—at the time.

"Yep. You have me dangling in the breeze, Cody."

She laughed again and I found I liked her laugh. It was . . . well, subdued, but genuine. Many salesmen don't have honest laughs, if one knows what to listen for. That little twinge of . . . whatever it was nudged me again. I pushed it away. Back then, I did not understand gentle proddings.

A few blocks from the rock joint, we found a small cafe and I asked if she was hungry. She was. And maybe, the thought came to me, she was carefully conserving her money. While I settled for coffee, I sat and marveled at the appetite of someone so dainty. She devoured two cheeseburgers, an order of fries, and two glasses of milk.

While she ate, I studied her face. It was a good, honest face, without blemish, her complexion smooth and still lightly tanned from the long summer's sun. I could find no fault with her. She was beautiful. That should have tipped me off right then that I was letting my emotions blindside me. Cody's hair was thick and shining with health. She wore little make-up; she didn't need any help in that department, or in any other, that I could see.

The waitress ambled over and asked if I or my daughter would like anything else. I could have cheerfully stuffed my coffee cup down her throat. Cody hid her smile behind a napkin while I ordered more coffee.

"We got some good apple pie," the waitress said.

I declined. Cody ordered a wedge.

"And put some ice cream on it, too," she called.

With my coffee cup filled and Cody attacking the pie and ice cream, I asked, "So tell me about Vic's boy. How far out of line did he get?"

"He finally realized that even with nine hands he wasn't going to get anywhere with me, so he asked if I'd like to smoke." She put those pale eyes on me and something unfamiliar and soft stirred deep inside. "You know what I mean?"

"I know."

"I never did do much of it. None, anymore. You smoke?"

"No. Never have. I used to smoke cigarettes. I quit those."

"Were you really a hero, Larry?"

"No more than any other guy in my team."

"Larry Bad-Ass, huh?"

"Not anymore."

"I don't believe that. Anyway, we lit up and started toking. Boy, was that bad timing. The cops came by where we were parked. It was really an ugly scene. But Mike's dad is the richest man in the county—maybe the richest in the state. The cops didn't know what to do. Vic Goodman owns the cops, Larry. He *owns* them. So they made us follow them to the mansion. It was then I found out what Mike is really made of. I mean, he's been smoking dope and dropping pills, all kinds, since he was in the eighth grade. He's a pusher, but you'll never convince Vic of that. Why, when Mike has all the money in the world, would he want to push drugs? It makes no sense to me. Anyway, Mikey-boy is the greatest thing since Jesus—according to his parents. Why are parents so stupid about their kids?"

"I don't know, Cody."

"Are you married? The talk around Pine Hills is that your wife is back in New York City."

"She's my ex-wife, Cody. We're divorced. No kids."

"Well, Mikey really put on a great performance that evening. I mean, it was Academy Awards night at the Goodman mansion, with tears and pointing fingers and the whole bit. The fingers, of course, were all pointing at me. Mike convinced his dad and the cops that the dope was mine. Said I'd teased him until he agreed to smoke with me. He said the only way I'd agree to have sex with him was if he used dope. Mike is, or was back then, a half-assed jock, and you know how some people look at jocks. Man, they can do no wrong."

I knew only too well. I had taken advantage of that misguided philosophy all through high school and college. But when I volunteered for a special ops unit, I found that my past exploits on the gridiron didn't spell jack-shit to those guys. If anything, I had to work harder to prove myself.

As Cody told her story—and I didn't doubt a word of it, knowing Vic—I began to notice little things about her. Her clothes were not new, and there were some very carefully mended places on her blouse. I'm very picky about my own clothes, and also very observant about what other people wear.

"So Vic blew up," Cody was saying. "I mean, he really unloaded on me. He even embarrassed the cops with some of the things he called me. What could I do?" She shrugged her slender shoulders. "I'm nothing in Pine Hills. My parents had just been killed in an accident. Mike was the first date I'd had since their deaths." She shook her head. "Anyway, I just stood there and took it until he ran out of steam. The cops took me home. One of them even apologized, then asked me to please not tell anybody that he did. He'd lose his job. That's how powerful Victor Goodman is. Well, the next afternoon it was all over town that I'm a dope-smoking, pill-popping, acid-taking, coke-sniffing whore. I'm glad my parents didn't have to hear those things. I hate the Goodmans—all of them—but I'm really afraid of Mike."

"Afraid of him? Why?"

"Why? Because Mike swore he'd get me for the things I said about him that night. But damn! I was only telling the truth. Mike's tried to run over me—twice. I'm serious; he has. I don't smoke anymore, either. Mike had one of his friends give me a couple of joints laced with PCP—a lot of it. Enough to put me spacey—permanently. He poisoned my little dog and I could kill him for that. He's tried to have me raped by some local thugs, but I'm pretty fast on my feet. I have to be very careful and walk light, Larry. Really light."

The girl was really boxed in. I knew Vic owned the local cops, and probably had a great deal of influence with the sheriff's department, too. Many small towns have a shadow government behind the elected officials, and in Pine Hills, that was Vic Goodman.

"What does your aunt think about the talk?"

Her eyes touched mine. "You really do know something about me, don't you, Larry?"

"Only what Vic told me that day."

"My aunt is kind of out of it, if you know what I mean. She wouldn't believe anything bad about me even if she understood what was being said. She knows me too well. She's senile, but harmless."

"And the money you get from your parents' insurance goes to help support your aunt, right?"

Her features tightened and her eyes narrowed. "You're very quick, aren't you, Mr. Baldwin?" Formal again. Two steps forward, one step back. "So what if it does? What's it to you, anyway?"

I held up a hand. Peace. "I'm just observant, Cody. That's all. I'm sorry if I offended you. I didn't mean to, believe me."

"Let's clear the air, Mr. Baldwin. There are a few things that I'm not going to do for a living, and a couple of them are being a barmaid in some damn Georgia honky-tonk and selling my butt. And that's about all the options that your Mr. Goodman has left me in this county. And I can't leave because I want to stay close so I can take care of my aunt. You see, even though it's illegal, any store who hires me loses trade from anyone employed by the Goodman Industries. Oh, yeah, that's right. At first some of his employees refused to go along with it. They either got fired or got the crap beat out of them by thugs that Victor keeps on the payroll to make sure his whores stay in line . . . and other really shitty little odd jobs. A couple of those employees sued. Guess what? The one case that did come to trial? The jury was out about five minutes. They ruled in favor of Vic Goodman. Big surprise? Not to me. Money spells power, and Vic Goodman has plenty of both." She then proceeded to call Vic a string of cuss words that would have awed my old drill sergeant, ending with, "Big, lard-assed, no-good, son of a bitch!"

Vic had been right on one point: Cody could lay down the profanity.

"So Vic really put the word out on you?"

Her face told the whole story. She toyed with her water glass. I suddenly realized that for some strange reason, I did not like to see her unhappy. It was a very odd sensation for me.

"What would you like to do, Cody? What do you do now to earn money?"

"I do odd jobs. I babysit for a lawyer in town who wouldn't spit on Vic Goodman if he was on fire. I work part-time at a little convenience store owned by a man who hates Vic Goodman almost as much as I do. And Vic's afraid, really afraid, to do anything about that job. Mr. Larsen is dying of cancer, and he told Vic, nose to nose, that before he dies, he'd like to do the world a favor and rid the earth of Victor Goodman. He'd do it, too. I mean, Mr. Larsen really might kill Vic before he dies. Vic has people watching Larsen.

"What I'd like to do? I'd like to go to college and get a degree . . . but for now, that's out of the question. My second choice is computer school here in Atlanta. If I had the money, which I don't." She sighed. "But, someone's got to look after Aunt Blanche, and I got elected."

"Bitter?"

Her face brightened. "Oh, no! Aunt Blanche is sweet and fun to be with. It's kind of sad, but even though she's getting worse, she's still all sorts of fun . . . most of the time. But she's so forgetful. One time she decided to fix supper. Chicken and dumplings. She had me get her a hen to stew. Then she forgot what she did with it. Next morning I got ready to take my bath and found it. She'd put it in the bathtub. You ever stepped on a naked chicken, Larry?"

I broke up with laughter, causing the other patrons in the cafe to turn and look at us. "No, Cody. I have to admit I've never stepped on a naked chicken. Who looks after your aunt while you're away?"

"The neighbors. People from the church. Really, I guess she's going to have to be put in a place where she can get constant care, but I don't like to think about that. She's all I have. I guess I'm kind of using her as a crutch to stay around Pine Hills."

I shook my head. "No, Cody. I don't think that's it at all. With your aunt in a nursing home, you'd have the money to go to school. You just care a great deal for her, that's all."

"Very quick, aren't you?"

I'm not—or wasn't back then—the kind of person who helped others. Charities had learned to take my name off their mailing lists. There was something in my bearing or in my eyes that made street people pull back their hands and close their mouths. But this young lady was having an effect on me that was baffling and I wasn't at all certain I liked the sensation.

"Well, Cody, maybe I could . . ."

Her eyes flashed pale blue fire. "Maybe you could do nothing! Maybe you could mind your own business! If the time ever comes when I want a Care package, I'll let you know. Okay, *Mister* Larry Baldwin?"

Quick on the trigger, too. "Sorry I offended you. I guess the holiday spirit got too much for me to handle."

"Uh-huh. Sure. And everybody who believes that can

jump up and sing Dixie." She pushed back her chair and stood up, pointing to the empty plates. "You paying for all this?"

"Sure. But you're wrong about me, Cody."

"Maybe. Maybe I am." The fire in her eyes faded a bit, the coals banked. "Maybe I'll see you around, sir. Thanks for the food." She turned to leave.

But I did not want her to leave. "Cody? Are you sure you have enough money for a taxi?"

Her smile was a curious one. A mixture of tenderness and surprise. She put out one small hand to touch my shoulder, then pulled it back at the last second. "Why don't you have any kids, Larry?"

I shrugged my shoulders. I really didn't know the answer. Or just wouldn't admit it.

"Too busy making money to fool with kids, huh?"

"Something like that, I suppose."

"Sure. Well, yeah, I have enough money for a cab. See you around, Larry."

Then she was gone, out the door and into the night, all five feet, two or three inches of her, long black hair flowing. I sat at the table by the window and watched her hail a passing cabby. She turned, looked back at me looking at her, and waved shyly. Then she was gone.

She had left a handkerchief on the table. I picked it up and fingered the fabric for a moment before putting it in the pocket of my custom tailored and very expensive suit. I put my fingers to my lips—the lingering scent of her had transferred from the linen to my fingers. I can still remember it.

I signaled to the waitress, then watched her walk slowly

over to the table. She wasn't unattractive, just tired-looking and discouraged. She looked like one of those people life had beaten down. Her feet probably hurt, too. I felt sorry for her.

Damn! What was the matter with me?

I paid the bill and then went back to the table and put a twenty-dollar bill by my coffee cup. The waitress's voice stopped me at the door.

"Hey, mister! You left a twenty. You know?"

"So keep it," I said, without turning around, then walked out into the night.

What a Boy Scout you are, Baldwin. Just full of the Christmas spirit.

I didn't sleep worth a damn that night, my sleep restless and dream-filled. I almost never remember my dreams, but these I remembered. They were of Cody, and that irritated me. I sat on the edge of the bed and cussed softly, disgusted with myself, but not for the right reasons. I cursed myself because I was almost forty-one years old and here I sat, mooning over some young piece.

"Damn, Larry!" I said. "You're pathetic!" I took a hot shower and went back to bed, managing to get a few hours sleep. But I still dreamed of Cody. The next morning, Atlanta seemed to have lost its charm. Unless . . .

"No, sir," the lady at the YW said. "Miss West checked out about an hour ago."

Crap.

I got my gear and drove back to Pine Hills. It was a cool, crisp, and clear day, but my weekend had soured. I knew what would get it back right. An hour and a half later, I was back in my office in the deserted Goodman Building, poring over figures and stats.

And I didn't think about Cody all day. Much.

I drove myself just as hard as I drove the staff for the first two weeks of December and spent a lot of time on the road and in the air, gearing up for the new year. I handled one especially difficult account in St. Louis—worth major bucks—and landed it. I could have taken the entire commission, since the area rep had backed out, considering it hopeless, and any other time I would have done just that. But I was feeling charitable, so I split it with him. Not that he deserved it. He didn't. He had almost blown the whole package. But what the hell? It was Christmas. Ho, ho, ho and all that.

While in St. Louis, I stopped in to see an old army buddy of mine. We'd spent a year together in Central America and he is one of the few close friends I have. He's an attorney, and a damned good one. I told him what I wanted, and then sat and watched a funny expression cross his face. I waited patiently for what I sensed was coming. I wasn't wrong.

"This is Larry Baldwin, isn't it?" he asked with a smile. "Ol' hard-assed, super-trooper, hard-chargin' Sergeant Baldwin? Are you real?"

"Get it all said, Louis. Get all the jokes over with. The kid's had—is having a bad time of it. I want to help." I really didn't know why I was doing this spur-of-the-moment thing. It was entirely out of character. But I couldn't get Cody out of my mind. Something about her fascinated me. Wrong word. Not *fascinate*, but *enchant*. Besides, I wanted to screw her.

"Uh-huh," Louis said drily.

"Look, Louis, I've got the money. I've been frugal most of my life and if I told you how much I'm worth, it would knock your socks off."

"All right, Larry." He held up a hand. "All right. How much money are we talking about?"

"Oh, four or five thousand dollars should put her through a good school in Atlanta. Year, eighteen months. A good computer school. Not some fly-by-night operation."

Louis looked at me for a long moment. He sighed. "Larry, we've been through some good times together, and a lot of really lousy times. El Salvador, Nicaragua . . . hell, your memory is as good as mine. Level with me. You're . . . what? Almost forty-one? Yeah. Is this one of those mid-life crisis things?"

"Hell, no!"

"Are you in love with this kid?"

That startled me—shook me badly for a few seconds. Love had not entered my mind. I had never experienced that and never planned to. Yes, I wanted to take the girl to bed, but I also genuinely liked Cody and felt sorry for her. Besides, a good romp in the sack never hurt anybody. I said as much to Louis.

"A five-thousand-dollar fuck?" he blurted.

"Oh, hell, Louis. My accountant will figure some way for me to take this off my tax."

"I repeat: are you in love with this kid?"

"I only met the girl one time, for Christ's sake. Love? That's stupid."

"Is it, Larry?" he asked softly. "Maybe not. You been to bed with her?"

I shook my head. "No. Louis, I haven't even kissed her. Or touched her. I want to help her, that's all."

But the handkerchief she had left at the table at the cafe in Atlanta was carefully tucked away in a dresser back in my house in Pine Hills. Twice I had thrown it away. Twice I had retrieved it, feeling a little foolish as I did.

Louis grinned at me. I remembered that grin well. "Well, Larry, we didn't kiss some of those hants we used to prong down in Central America, either. Remember?"

"I'm trying to forget all that. Louis, all kidding aside, can you fix this thing up for me, or not?"

Again, he sighed. "I . . . don't know. Any way I go will be chancy, at best. Do you even know the name of a good school there?"

"Hell, no. Call the chamber of commerce. There must be several schools there. One of them has to be good. Just find the best one and take it from there."

"Larry, is this girl stupid?"

"No. What the hell kind of question is that?"

He stared at me and drummed his fingertips on the desktop. "Did you approach her with an offer of help?"

"I started to."

"And she turned you down?"

"Cold. Angrily." I thought back to that night and for a moment, her image dimmed everything in the office as the scent of her entered my brain. I drifted off.

"Larry!" Louis's voice jarred me back to reality.

"I'm right here."

"Dammit, Larry, pay attention to me. I think I was right. If you aren't in love, you sure have all the symptoms. You remind me of me when I was in the eighth grade and fell in love with Miss O'Malley. Now, are you back with me for a few more minutes?"

"Yes, Lieutenant." I grinned at him, feeling a bit foolish. But he was wrong about love. I was certain of that. I just wanted to help Cody out and then bed her down, that's all.

"Look, understand this," he said drily. "She's probably going to smell a rat and toss the whole package right back in your foolish face."

"So? You're a devious fellow. You'll think of something, I'm sure."

Louis sighed and looked pained. "All right, all right. Get out of here. I'll take care of it—somehow."

But when I returned to Pine Hills in the middle of December, I learned that Cody had been picked up on a dope charge and was cooling her butt in the county jail.

 *Four*

I knew I was going to have to handle this very carefully. I could not get openly involved. If Vic ever found out I had interceded in Cody's behalf, I would be in deep trouble. So I went to the attorney I had retained in Pine Hills to handle any personal business I might have. I dumped it in Tom Vanderwedge's lap.

"You work for Vic Goodman and you want to help Cody West?" he questioned. "Why?"

"I don't like Vic Goodman. But his money spends real well."

Tom smiled. "Yeah. All right. I'll accept that for the moment . . . and keep your name out of it. It's a nothing charge, Larry. My kids say it was Mike Goodman who tipped the cops that she was carrying and they stopped her on his word alone. That in itself is a violation of her rights because Mike is on record as having turned Cody in about five dozen times and each time turned out to be false. The police had no real probable cause, no warrant. What they have her on is resisting arrest, disturbing the peace, nit-picking charges. What made it so bad is she started cussing and hollering. Cody's got a bad mouth on her when she gets wound up. And she really let the cops have it this time, kicking and screaming. Well," he sighed, "she wasn't carrying any dope. But the cops hit her several times. I'm not saying they were right or wrong; she was fighting them. Maybe they could have handled it differently. Hell, I know they could. If that had been the mayor's wife or kid, or some city councilman's kid . . . well, you know the drill."

"Only too well, Tom."

"I have spoken with the chief of police. I informed him that Cody will be released, promptly, with all charges dropped and no record or I'll sue the shit out of that department. I don't have Vic Goodman's money—who does?—but my great-grandfather settled this town. The founding family and all that. That's a statue of him on the courthouse lawn. Goddammit!" he roared, slamming a hand down on the desk.

"Did they mark her, Tom?"

"Oh, hell, yes. One side of her face is all swelled up. Bruised. I feel so damned sorry for her."

So did I. I fought back hot anger until it cooled into the icy kind. "Names of the arresting officers, Tom?"

The lawyer looked at me for a moment. "Simmons and Barlow. You watch your step, Larry. They're rough."

I smiled at him and tossed a signed check onto his desk. "Just get her out, Tom."

Cody appeared at my door at seven o'clock that evening, leaning on the doorbell until I answered it. Cold fury washed over me at the sight of her. It looked as though the cops had gone to work on her with a calculated vengeance. The right side of her face was bruised from forehead to chin. The eye was swelled shut.

Merry Christmas, Little Cody West. All five feet, three inches of you. Maybe a hundred pounds. Merry Christmas from the Pine Hills Police Department. Bought and paid for and solely owned by Victor Goodman.

"I won't come in, Larry Baldwin," she said. "That would get you in trouble with asshole Goodman."

"Vic's out of town. Entertaining the French with his charming colloquialisms. Hell with him. Come on in, it's freezing out. Cody, did you walk all the way over here?"

"Of course not. I rode my magic carpet. Didn't you hear me land on the roof?" She stepped inside and I closed the door.

Her face looked even rougher in the light—yellow and green all mixed in with the dark purple and blue. And I got pissed. I've handled very dangerous and professional guerrilla fighters without inflicting that much damage. My anger must have registered on my face.

She gently touched my arm. Her hand was even bruised. "Let it alone, Larry. You probably won't, but I wish you would. I just stopped by to thank you for helping to get me out. I've taken several baths but I still can smell that damn jail. Mister Vanderwedge told me what you did, but he didn't tell anyone else, and won't. He's a nice man and boy, was he mad. He told those cops how the cow ate the cabbage."

I waved her to a chair. "Sit down, Cody. Relax. How many times did the cops hit you, and with what, for Christ's sake?"

"Five or six times, with a leather thing and with their fists.

That I can remember, that is. They knocked me out." Before she sat down, she pulled up one side of her jacket and shirt. "They kicked me, too."

Black and blue and purple marred her soft skin. I felt sick at my stomach. She was so little. I slowly unclenched my fists.

"Mister Vanderwedge says all police charges have been dropped and the city will pay for any medical treatment, and he says I'm going to the doctor about a hundred and twenty-eight times, at least. All I had to do was sign a statement releasing the department from fault, or something like that."

"You didn't sign the goddamn thing, did you?"

"Larry, you don't understand. Victor Goodman owns the police, the sheriff, and the deputies of this county. He owns the largest factory here. He employs a lot of people. He owns the motel, the mall, the bank, the theater. He owns everything, Larry. And he owns a lot of the people, too. Half the population works for Vic Goodman, in one way or the other. Believe it."

I nodded my understanding. "Can I get you something to drink?"

"Coke, I guess."

"Anything in it?"

She shook her head, slowly. She probably had a headache. "No, the good fairy would revoke my magic carpet privileges if I drink and fly."

I grinned at her and headed for the wet bar. She still had a sense of humor. She looked around the den. The house is lovely, sitting on three acres of land in a very exclusive part of town. It came furnished and most of it is expensive and in good taste.

Cody looked at the fireplace and studied the dancing flames. "It's very nice," she said. "I guess you worked hard to get all this."

"It isn't mine." I handed her the Coke over ice. "It belongs to the company. It's just one of the luxuries that go with the job."

"It's beautiful." Her eyes were sad. "You don't pay any rent?"

I shook my head. "No. And I don't pay for that Cadillac parked in the drive, either."

She sipped her soft drink and looked at me. Even battered and bruised she was lovely. At least to my mind. And that should have been the tip-off and the cue for me to back away and do it quickly. I guess I was a little slow on the uptake. "Oh, yeah, Larry. You pay for them. You really do."

"Oh? How so?" But I knew.

"With your soul. You sell your soul to an asshole like Vic Goodman, that's how. And you know it. And that is, as far as I'm concerned, too high a price."

I sat down on the coffee table in front of her. "How do you know I'm not like Vic Goodman, Cody? Tell me, what do you really know about me? I'd like to know—like to know what you think. I can't read you very well."

Even with the side of her face looking like Quasimodo's hump, she managed a smile. "And you don't like that, do you, Larry Baldwin?"

"No. I don't. Reading people is part of my job."

"Yeah. I thought so. Well, I know you're a man who would like everybody to fear him. That's the talk around town. And I guess you've succeeded. People say you're ruthless, savage, tough, and have no heart. All that is probably true to some degree. But you know what, Larry Baldwin? I think you're a lonely man. Whether you'll admit it or not. I think it's lonely where you are, up here in this ivory tower. And I'll tell you something else: I don't know just exactly what my feelings are about you. Two days ago, when I received a letter concerning a special scholarship to the most expensive business school in Atlanta, I would have gladly slapped your face. If you think you can buy me into your bed, you're very, very wrong."

She was one sharp young lady. She had me pegged cold. I started to protest, pointing my finger at her. She held up a small hand, silencing me. "Don't point your finger at me, Larry. I don't like that."

"Sorry," I muttered.

"And then what you did this morning really blew my mind. Are you nuts, Larry? Don't you realize if word of this gets out, Butthole Goodman will fire you? He hates me, Larry. He despises me. And I'll tell you something else: I don't think you really know who you are. I don't believe you've ever found the real Larry Baldwin. I think he's locked up inside you somewhere. You're afraid to let your feelings show. You must have had a pretty shitty childhood, Larry. Either that, or you've taken some rough knocks through the years."

She had put some pegs into the right holes. And her accuracy was slightly irritating. How could one so young know so much. Was I that easy to read? "Are you all through?"

"For the time being."

"More Coke?"

She shook her head. "No comment on what I just said?"

"No. Not at this time. Maybe later. Are you going to go to school, Cody?"

"Not with your money."

"There are no strings attached."

She smiled. "Oh, yeah, Larry. There are strings dangling everywhere. Maybe five thousand dollars isn't much to you, but it is to me. Larry, you don't even know me! This is only the second time we've talked. How many times have you done something like this?"

"First time."

She shook her head—again, carefully—and searched my face with her eyes. "Maybe you're just plain bonkers."

I laughed at that. "No. I don't think so, Cody. At least not any more than others in this crazy business."

"Well, anyway, some good news. I got a job. Finally. I start the first of the year. The new factory just out of town. I'll be doing office work. It's just a bit over the minimum wage, but they say if I do well, I'll get a raise."

"Your aunt?"

"Neighbors will look after her. She's all right by herself. They'll see that she doesn't wander off."

"You'll do well at the plant. Is it the subsidiary of the Huttle Company?"

"Yeah. That's it."

"I know the plant manager. They brought him in from New York. Bernie will tell Vic to kiss off if he starts any crap about you. I'll make sure of that." But I didn't tell her about the reports that the company was in trouble nationally. They were sinking slowly into the red and this was a desperation move on their part.

"Okay," she agreed. "You can do that for me, long as I got the job on my own. But you don't do or say anything else unless I come and ask you."

"Deal."

She finished her drink and limped to the door. I suspected she had been kicked in the legs. There was no doubt she was in pain. Simmons and Barlow would be, too, if the opportunity ever presented itself. She turned at the door and took an envelope from her purse, laying it on the foyer table. "Merry Christmas, Larry Baldwin."

Then she was gone into the cold darkness.

I stood by the window, watching her limp down the street. Then, as she had done in Atlanta, she stopped, turned around, and waved shyly at me. I returned the wave.

Opening the envelope, I smiled at the Christmas card. It was handmade. She had drawn a cartoon depicting a small but well-endowed young lady standing in front of a tall man in a business suit. It was a pretty fair likeness of both of us. The caption read: BUT SIR, I'LL HAVE YOU KNOW I'M A GOOD GIRL!

No doubt about it, I had met a genuine character.

But I still intended to take her to bed.

For some reason, this holiday season affected me more than any other in memory. I have never been a sentimental person, but this Christmas and New Year's Eve really got to me. I was alone, by my own choosing . . . and lonely. Being alone had never bothered me before. But this season it did, cutting into me like a dull knife.

My thoughts invariably returned to Cody, no matter how

hard I tried to push them away. No doubt about it—I was obsessed with her. But one thing continued to puzzle me: I had made it with many women, and carefully charted out the campaign to do so, but none had ever stayed on my mind. I didn't understand what was taking place inside my head. It never dawned on me that what was happening was taking place in my heart.

I would have rejected that immediately.

I didn't see Cody for almost a month, and then it was by accident. I had stopped at a local club after work—a members-only place—and saw her with a tall, good-looking young man. I felt as though I had been kicked in the guts. She waved and came over, dragging him with her. She introduced me and chatted for a time. I could tell he was less than thrilled. I forgot his name immediately, all my attention riveted on Cody. She was beautiful, all the bruises from the beating gone.

The young man said, at least twelve times, "Uh . . . Cody." Either his conversational abilities were extremely limited or he was severely retarded. He kept flexing his muscles and giving me dirty looks. If he was trying to frighten me, he was doing a lousy job of it. I saw at least a dozen opportunities to ruin his spleen, rupture his larynx, break his nose, and tear off his lower lip. It would have taken all of three seconds. Hard training never really leaves a person. You just learn to control it.

Cody searched my face for a few seconds and then it dawned on her that I was uncomfortable.

"I'll see you, Larry," she said brightly.

"All right, Miss West." I did not mean it to sound so stuffy. I just wanted to defuse what was quickly developing into a bad situation.

Hurt sprang into her eyes and I felt like a jackass. She turned away, her Neanderthal companion in tow.

Then I saw Patrolman Simmons walk in, all dressed up in civilian clothes. There was a bulge in his jacket that told me he was carrying a pistol in a shoulder rig. Tom Vanderwedge suddenly appeared at my side, a drink in his hand.

"Don't do it, Larry," he said quietly.

"You a mind reader, Tom?"

"No. But I saw the look on your face when Simmons walked in. Just back off."

"Yeah, you're right. This isn't the place."

Cody and Jungle Jim had disappeared into the crowd and Tom sat with me at the bar and chitchatted until Simmons left. He didn't stay long. No one in the club seemed to want to associate with him. Tom walked with me out to the car. "You take it easy now, Larry," he cautioned. "Believe me, Chief Pardue got his ass in a crack over what happened to Cody. A lot of townspeople came down hard on him. It'll never happen again."

"All right, Tom. And thanks."

That was on a Friday evening. Saturday afternoon, about three, Cody called the house.

"I just want to tell you that you were a genuine prick last night, Larry Baldwin," she said. One thing about Cody, she came right to the point, all social amenities aside.

"Yeah? Well . . . maybe. But it was getting to be a bad scene. Are you waiting for an apology?"

"Only if it's sincere."

I said nothing.

"I see," she whispered. "Well, I've learned something else about you."

"Oh? And that is?"

She sidestepped the question. "Larry, what's wrong? I thought you were my friend."

"I am your friend, Cody. Believe it." A friend that wants to take you to bed.

"Well, you sure as hell didn't much act like a friend last night."

"Cody, your speech-impaired companion was flexing his muscles and giving me very dirty looks."

"To hell with him! There's nothing between Andy and me. I'll talk with my friends any damn time I feel like it. Nobody tells me what to do or who I can talk with."

"Okay, okay, Cody. Calm down. How are you doing? How's the job? I haven't seen you in a month."

"You saw me last night."

"That is not what I mean and you know it."

She was silent for several heartbeats. I'd bet her face was a real study. "You having any company tonight, Larry?"

"Nope."

"Going to be all alone, huh?"

"Yep."

"You mind if I come visit you?"

My heart skipped about two beats. "That would be very nice, Cody." I did my best to keep my tone level. "Would you like me to fix dinner?"

"No. Nothing like that."

Like what, then? "I'm afraid the records I have are pretty outdated."

"I like most kinds of music."

"All right."

"The neighbors might talk, Larry," she teased.

"Hell with the neighbors. My friends can come over to my house any damn time they please."

She laughed. "Calm down, Larry. I'll see you tonight. 'Bout seven."

And that was how the wind blew the butterfly into my life.

 *Five*

After a careful shower and shave, I stood in my drawers wondering what I should wear. What does a forty-year-old man wear when entertaining a twenty-one-year-old lady? I could say quite truthfully that I had never had to deal with that question before. I had not been a jeans addict in years— except tight-fitting ones on ladies—and didn't even own a pair. I finally dressed in an old pair of army khakis and an L.L. Bean shirt that was one of my favorites, then slipped into loafers. I honest-to-God felt like a kid. Good, happy. It was the strangest damned sensation, and I wondered about it while fixing a drink.

I've dated some of the best-looking women to be found anywhere, and my address book is filled with names and numbers. But there I was, acting like a fool simply because a certain young lady was coming to see me. A young lady I had never touched, never kissed. Weird, Larry, weird. And not at all like me. Larry Baldwin thought everything through very carefully, mapped out all the options, then chose the best plan, complete with escape routes.

Well, I thought, so let's map it out, then, because getting Cody into bed was what this was all about.

I stood for a moment in the bedroom, thinking about that. Somehow it didn't ring true. The note was discordant. So what, then, was happening? Was the old Larry changing? If so, was the change for the better?

Maybe I would know the answer to that before the night was over.

The doorbell chimed and I wanted to run to answer it. Settle down, Larry. Settle down. I gathered up my composure, sorted out all my emotions, then carefully tucked them into their proper niches in my mind.

I began the walk to the front door; damn, but this was a big house. My lawyer-buddy's words echoed in my mind: *Mid-life crisis. You in love with the girl, Larry? You been to bed with her?*

I hung a smile on my face and opened the door.

Victor Goodman stood on the porch, grinning at me like a big ugly toad.

Jesus Christ! what a letdown. Expect Beauty and get the Beast.

"Hi, there, Larry-boy!" he boomed. "Me and the old lady just got back into town and I wanted to come over and shake and howdy with you. You lookin' fat and sassy, boy."

I recovered nicely and shook his hand, then waved him inside, hoping he would decline the offer.

He came in. "I cain't stay long, boy. I just wanted to see you and get a quick rundown on how things have been goin' whilst I been gone over yonder listenin' to all that Frog jibber-jabber."

I just bet Ol' Vic was a pure delight amid the Parisians.

I asked the expected. "How about something to drink, Vic?"

"No, no." He waved the offer aside. "Me and my old woman ain't even et yet, boy, and I ain't even gonna sit down."

Thank God for little favors.

"You know what I want, Larry-boy. Just give it to me short and sweet and profitable."

"The last quarter of year ending was up, December the best in five years, and January, so far, is running six percent over last year."

"Hot damn! That's the best Christmas present a man could get." He slapped me on the back and I moved toward the door. He followed, then stopped, his little piggy eyes narrowing a bit. "You wouldn't be tryin' to get rid of the boss, now, would you, Larry-boy?"

I smiled and winked at him. His whole hog face lit up as he got the message. "Whoo-boy! I got you now. You expectin' a woman out here, huh? Well, hell, never let it be said that ol' Vic ever stood 'tween a man and his pussy." He leaned close and said, "Local gal?"

"She's from Atlanta, Vic. I've got to go meet her and bring her here." The lies came so effortlessly.

He looked at me from loafers to old shirt and shook his head. "You shore dressed funny to be meetin' up with a city woman. How old is she, nineteen?"

I laughed my best salesman's laugh and Vic joined in. "What the hell would I do with a nineteen-year-old, Vic?"

He punched me on the shoulder and grinned lewdly. "Why, hell's-fire, Larry-boy, that's the best snatch in the world. It ain't had time to get all wallered out. See you Monday morning." He stopped, turned around, and looked back at me, standing in the door. "Larry, you heard anythin' about my boy, Mike?"

I shook my head and in the process my eyes caught a shape standing in the bushes on the south end of the house. Cody. She was standing with her arms folded under her breasts, smiling at me. Jesus! If Vic turned the wrong way . . . "No, Vic. I haven't heard a word about Mike. Is something the matter?"

"Naw." He took a step and leaned against the doorjamb. "Not really. I just heard some talk about that trashy West gal, that's all. Somethin' about Mike tippin' off the po-lice 'bout her sellin' some dope, or somethin' like 'at."

I shook my head. "No. I haven't heard anything about that. But I've been spending a lot of time on the road. And I don't socialize much here in Pine Hills. I just don't get a chance to hear much gossip."

"Yeah, that's right. I forgot—all work and no play for Larry-boy." He winked. " 'Ceptin' for tonight, that is. Chief Pardue stopped me on the way over here, told me that when his boys grabbed her, she fought 'em hard and they had to smack her around some. Knocked her out, cold as a hammer. But that ain't all." He laughed, and it was dirty-sounding. "The cops that grabbed her, Simmons and Barlow, both of them got some pretty good feels of them titties of hers whilst she was in the back seat. Said them titties was nice. Said she was unconscious. But I bet you she wasn't no such of a thing. I bet you she was wide awake and lovin' ever' second of it.

"I know women, Larry. And I been around enough to know

'bout them women that holler rape all the time. And I know trash, too. And that West gal is pure trash. Well, I'll see you, Larry-boy. You have fun tonight and don't get none on you, now, you hear?"

He walked to his car without looking back, chuckling down the sidewalk. I began to breathe a bit easier when his taillights had turned the corner and disappeared.

I glanced at Cody. She was standing outside of the bushes now, giving Vic the middle-finger with both hands, sticking out her tongue, and making some really horrible faces as he drove away. Then she made a very profane hand gesture.

"That is a male gesture, dear," I told her. "Females do it much differently."

"How would you know?" she popped right back. "Never mind." She stuck her tongue out at me.

"My grandmother used to tell me—when she would catch me making faces—what a tragedy it would be if my face froze like that forever. Come on in the house, Cody. It's cold out here."

She was furious as she brushed past me and into the house, eyes flashing blue fire. Furious or not, she still smelled good and I inhaled the scent of her deeply.

"I figured those damn redneck cops were probably up to no good. My jeans were unzipped and my shirt open when I came to in that stinking cell. How sick can people get? That damn Simmons used to bug me to go out with him. Even threatened to arrest me if I didn't. I hope he got his hands full, 'cause that's the only time he'll ever put them on me."

I would deal with Simmons and Barlow, sooner or later. I was sure of that. But for now, I thought, the best thing to do was keep my mouth shut and let Cody get it all out of her system. And that she did.

I sat in a chair and sipped my drink, watching her pace the carpet, waving her slender arms and calling Vic and Mike some extremely choice names.

"That no-good, half-assed jock bastard. Telling his father he made out with me. That's low, Larry—really low. Mike is the last person on the face of the earth I would let make love to me . . ."

I wondered who was number one? That hairy jungle-type with the limited conversational ability?

I shuddered at the thought.

She finally ran out of steam and plopped down on the couch and glared at me.

I smiled at her. She was so beautiful. "Don't be angry at me, Cody. I didn't do anything." I mentally amended that statement.

"I know it, Larry. I'm sorry I yelled at you. You're just so calm all the time and I needed someone to yell at."

"Any time." And I meant it.

We looked at each other for a moment.

"How about something to drink?" I suggested.

"Sure. That'd be great. You have any wine?"

"Certainly." I told her what I had in the wine rack and she grimaced.

"I mean some real drinking wine."

I didn't know what she meant. "But, Cody, that's what I just said."

"No, Larry," she corrected with a smile, the curve of her lips capable of melting ice. "I mean some sweet wine. Drink-in' kind." She named a brand that I wouldn't have given my drill sergeant. And there were times I would have gladly given him hemlock.

It was my turn to grimace. "God, Cody. You don't actually drink that stuff, do you?"

"Sure. It's good."

"Okay. You wait here and I'll go get you some of that . . . wine."

"No, no, Larry. Not tonight. Tell you what: you have any beer?"

"Oh, sure." I named off several imported brands and my favorite from Germany. I was a bit crestfallen when she laughed.

"Hey, Larry! Come on back to earth, will you? How about just plain ol' beer?"

Muttering under my breath, I managed to round up a stray can of local beer, left in the house by the previous owner. It was on the back porch, so it was cold. If his taste in beer was any indication of his ability to sell, I had little doubts why Vic canned him.

Back in the den, I said, "That's the only can of that particular brand left in the house. Thank God," I added.

She laughed and waved away the glass I offered her. Then she knocked back about half the contents. "You do have bourbon, don't you?"

"Oh, yes. Plenty of that. And tomorrow I shall lay in a stock of your wine and beer."

"Why?" she asked. She sprawled on the couch, in her jeans and checkered shirt. She looked good enough to eat.

"Well, Cody . . . is this your first and last visit?"

She cocked her head to one side in that peculiar way of hers and those pale eyes found me, locking me in blue. "Why would you want me to come back, Larry?"

"I like your company."

"How old are you, really?"

"I'll be forty-one next month."

"What date?"

"The fourteenth."

"I'll be twenty-two the month after that. My ID was correct."

"What date?"

"The tenth."

"Then I shall be certain to get you something nice for that auspicious occasion."

Her eyes narrowed in suspicion.

I smiled at her. "Like a six-pack of that dreadful beer you drink."

The misgivings left her eyes. "I never had a real friend who was forty years old," she said.

"Don't trust anyone over thirty, is that it?"

"There is some truth to that, Larry."

"You'll be thirty someday. Cody, is my generation all that bad? I find that hard to believe. I thought people your age were all truth and light and love and trust?"

"Where'd you hear that shit? You're a little behind the times. The peace and love generation was in the sixties, maybe the early part of the seventies. I wasn't even born then!"

But I was. I was fighting a secret war and then beginning my climb up the corporate ladder. I had been in and out of several countries in Central America and killed two or three dozen men before this girl was out of diapers. Suddenly, I felt very old and foolish and worldly. I sighed heavily.

"Your face is changing, Larry. Again. What's the matter? What are you thinking?"

"Nothing of any importance."

"You're lying, Larry," she whispered, and I found myself flung back to that noisy bar in Atlanta. Damn! Was this girl omniscient? I knew very well I had a good poker face and could be hard to read. Was I so relaxed, so changed in her presence, that my guard was down? If so, then she was indeed an exceptional person.

I would learn later on just how exceptional.

I leveled with her, sort of. "I was thinking about the differences in our ages."

"Nineteen years."

"That's a lot of years, Cody."

"Depends on the people involved. But I guess it is, if that sort of thing bothers you."

"You don't mind having a friend who's nineteen years older?"

"Does it bother you?"

"Not in the least."

"So, Larry," Cody said. "Why don't you fix us a drink and we'll toast to our new friendship."

Drinks fixed, we clinked glasses solemnly. "To friendship," I said.

"I think we're going to be good friends, Larry. I think you're okay."

If only we had left it right there.

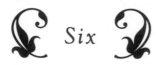

Six

I had to go out of town for almost a month, but while I was gone, Tom Vanderwedge was busy buying a place for me a few miles outside of town. His instructions had been simple and direct.

"I want a house that's secluded—very private. Lots of trees. And no neighbors."

Like any good lawyer, he asked no questions that weren't pertinent. "That won't be difficult, Larry. I know exactly what you're looking for and where it is. A dandy place for you to unwind." Sort of what I had in mind. "The place belongs to an old couple who never use it anymore. I'm their attorney. They've been trying to sell it for a couple of years. One big bedroom, huge den with a fireplace, good kitchen, and a utility room with washer and dryer. It's a couple of acres, I believe. Has a fence all around it and the lawn is covered with trees. House sits 'way back from the blacktop. Nearest neighbor is about a quarter of a mile. But the place needs some work. Nothing major, just the normal things that happen to a place that's been neglected for a couple of years."

He asked if I wanted to see the house and land and I said no. I trusted his judgment. Then we talked price for a few minutes and finally settled on what a local real estate man had said it was worth. I gave Tom power of attorney and signed a couple of checks on a New York bank.

"Get the carpenters working as soon as possible, Tom. Lay in a cord of firewood and top off the butane tank. I'll be in touch with you from the road. Probably once a week or so. You draw me a map showing where the place is, and I'll drive out there when I leave here. But I'm sure it's just what I want."

Then I wrote out a third check, payable to him, and he stared at it for a moment. "And this check, Larry?"

"Client-attorney relationship?"

"You don't even have to ask that. It won't leave this room."

"If you think this might put you in a bad light, Tom, you can back off and there'll be no hard feelings."

"I can't possibly imagine what that might be. Let me be the judge of that. What do you have on your mind?"

I sure as hell wasn't going to tell him that. "I've gotten to know Cody West since her, ah, little run-in with what passes for law in this town. I like the kid."

"Cody's a good kid. Kind of a free spirit. But basically she's a good, decent person." He smiled. "But my God, can she cuss."

"Yes, I found that out. And something else: Victor Goodman hates her."

"Screw Vic Goodman," he said, quite uncharacteristically.

"I know you work for him, but he's a goddamn redneck with money. And that's the worst kind of redneck."

I hid a smile, knowing I had found my man. Not everyone in Pine Hills just loved ol' Vic.

"What about Cody?" he prompted.

"She's been looking for a good secondhand car, but can't get financing because she hasn't been working long enough to establish a good credit record. She's been over at Benson Motors looking at some little car. I really don't know what make or model. Benson told me it's two years old and in fine shape. Low mileage. I'd like you to have a mechanic check it out. Then, the next time she's over there, she can discover that financing is now available."

"Financing available? How?" Tom looked worried.

"You've got it in your hand," I told him.

Tom looked at the check made out to him. "Ah. Now I'm with you."

"Correct. Benson will go along with it. He's a crusty old bastard, but he keeps his mouth shut and he likes Cody and dislikes Vic Goodman. He brought this up with me after I stopped over there looking for a secondhand pickup truck." Not exactly a lie. "He knows how Vic's punk kid put the mouth on Cody and would like to see her get this little car. But he didn't quite know how to pull it off."

"I . . . see. I think. Larry, am I allowed a personal question or two about this . . . deal?"

"Sure. Ask."

"Your reputation preceded you here, Larry. The Goodman Company is worth millions, but Pine Hills is a small town. All that wealth can, won't, buy silence for its top people. You played football for Georgia, and you're anything but unknown in the state. You're a decorated soldier. You're known in the business world as a ruthless, tough, coldhearted son of a bitch. You climbed to the top in a few short years. I've heard you've made some very shrewd and very risky moves in the investment field . . . that paid off big. You're worth a lot more than even Vic Goodman suspects. I've spoken with your attorney in New York City. I know your ex-wife didn't want any cash settlement."

He waited for one long moment for my reply. He got a little nervous. Finally, I said, "No, Tom. She didn't want anything from me. She just wanted out and away from me and I felt the same about her. It was a bad situation. She said we had no love to give each other; and that was true. She . . ."

He waved me silent, a pained look on his face. "That's terribly personal, Larry, and really none of my business. Point I'm making, or attempting to make, is: this car business now, that's not like you. It's all out of character. I find it odd. So I'm going to tell you something. I like Cody. I've known her since she was born. I was very close to her parents. I went to school with both of them—all the way through, from first grade through high school. My wife and I socialized with them. Cody's a good kid. So, mister, if you've got something in the back of your mind, some sort of sordid affair—I'll do my best to whip your ass!"

I stared at him for a moment, then burst out laughing. I just couldn't help it. Tom Vanderwedge is a very skinny five feet, seven inches—and that would be stretching it. After standing in a downpour, he might weigh a hundred and thirty. He can't see without his glasses, and a good wind would sail him to the state line. But he sure as hell wasn't short on guts.

I wiped my eyes with a handkerchief and was still chuckling as I looked at Tom across his neat desk. "Tom, you're a good man. I like you, and I don't say that to very many people. I'll level with you. I like Cody and I feel sorry for her. I helped her land the job she has now." Which wasn't a lie, but Cody didn't know anything about it. "I have never touched the kid and don't have any plans to do so. She's . . . well, sort of like the daughter I never had but always wanted. But I think I'd beat her butt for cussing the way she does. If she were mine, that is."

That brought a smile from him, just like I knew it would. Just keep on selling, Larry. The fish likes the bait and is eyeballing it. He's just about ready to suck it in like a big ol' bass. Then all you have to do is set the hook and land him.

"And I would like to help her in any way I can." I told him about my clumsy attempt to get her into a school in Atlanta.

He nodded and cleared his throat. "That was a hell of a nice gesture, Larry. I'm glad you told me about it." There was a definite catch in his voice.

Got him.

"Cody," I said, "well, she's such an idealistic rainbow in this cutthroat world that . . . just being around her puts me in a different mood. Do you know what I mean, Tom?"

Tom slowly nodded his head with a very sheepish look. "Yes, Larry, I do. You've put my mind at ease. I'm sorry for the things I said and thought. You're a good man, Larry."

Reeled him in and gutted him.

We shook hands and I left to drive by the country house.

I was such a charming and convincing liar.

I made all the stops on this tour. We've got outlets and reps in every state, and I saw nearly all of them, many times meeting them in an airport conference room between flights for a quick little pep talk from the boss.

But it was at night, alone in the hotel or motel room, that I felt the distance, my thoughts always returning to Cody. I was obsessed with her. That's what I called it. Then. I wanted her more than I had ever wanted any woman. I had never met a woman who so haunted me, and I could not understand it. The country was full of beautiful women. So why Cody?

I just didn't know. Then. But my heart knew. If only I had listened to it.

I was in the Northwest the second week of my tour and just couldn't take it any longer. I called Cody from Portland, Oregon. The neighbor who was staying with her aunt answered the phone. No, Cody was not at home. She was in Atlanta with a friend.

What friend?

She couldn't recall. Oh, yes! Andy something or another.

The Neanderthal.

I thanked her and hung up.

Depression hit me hard. I showered, shaved, dressed, and went out to have a few drinks. I decided to walk.

For a while it was a pleasant stroll, the night air tasting good. But old habits die hard and I found myself being followed by three men. Young men, by the way they moved and dressed. Once, when I stopped to straighten my tie in the reflection of a storefront window, I saw them to be in their early-to-mid-twenties. Punk types. Having a few drinks was pushed far back into my mind. In one sense, this was going to be a lot more fun.

I just don't like punks. I totally reject all that crap from the mouths of bleeding hearts. Some of the finest and most successful people I know came from childhoods of heartbreaking poverty. And they didn't steal or kill to get where they are. They worked a full-time job and two part-time jobs, seven days a week, and went to school the rest of the time, sleeping whenever they could find a spare moment. They worked, they read, they studied. They taught themselves self-discipline and set a goal and went after it. And they didn't make excuses or blame society.

Come on, you turd-heads, make your move.

The punks paced me, across the street, to my right. When one of them fell back, crossing the street, coming up behind me, staying about twenty meters to my rear, I knew they were setting me up for a mugging. I smiled behind a surge of anticipation. Providing, of course, they used clubs or knives, not guns.

Adrenaline began pumping through my veins. Years back I had found that I liked action, the meaner the better. The few fights I had in school—before the word spread to leave Larry Baldwin the hell alone—had been quick and brutal, with the other guy usually getting some bones broken or his balls kicked up into his belly. I never started a fight, which, I'm sure, had something to do with keeping me out of jail as a young person. But I would not then nor now be crowded by punks. Football helped take the edge off in high school and college and then working with a spec ops group honed it further. But I'll admit it: I like to mix it up every now and then.

"Come on, shit-heads," I muttered.

There was no traffic on the street I chose to turn down. No stores open. Near the middle of the pavement the streetlamp was out, and I knew that was where the punks would make their move.

Years back, I had taken to the army's unarmed combat schools like a kid reaching for the cookie jar. I loved every dirty minute of it and learned how to really fight, how to cripple, how to do it all with my hands. I learned the rough, savage, no-quarter crippling methods of staying alive. But more importantly, I had the mind-set to use it.

And now I was about to get another chance.

Three steps away from the darkened area around the dead streetlamp, by the yawning gloom of an alley, I heard the punk behind me come up in a rush. I turned to face him, seeing about eighteen inches of chain in his hand, just as the footsteps of his two dick-headed friends broke into a run in my direction.

He started to swing the chain, nervous and off-balance and startled because I was suddenly facing him, looking at him eyeball to eyeball, a strange smile on my lips. I stepped in close and effectively blocked the chain, at the same time driving my fingers into the softness of his throat. He gagged and dropped the chain just as I smashed his nose with the heel of my left hand and, using my right fist, hit him over the heart just as hard as I could. He dropped like a rock.

A knife flashed in the gloom as I dropped into a crouch and scooped up the chain, coming up with it and swinging it hard.

The chain caught the knife-user in the face and laid him wide open from hairline to tip of jaw. He screamed in agony and joined his worthless buddy on the sidewalk. The knife clattered away. The third street slime went into a panic and tried to run, but I blocked his way, a building to his back.

"Man!" he panted. "You let me go and I won't tell the cops what you done."

That's the mentality of the street punks these days. They know they have more rights than the victim. This punk knew that after this was over, he could find a crappy-enough lawyer to take his case, stack the jury with liberals and other assorted space-cadets, and win a sizeable judgment against me. Such is the sadness of our present criminal justice system.

I laughed at him and then drop-kicked his nuts up into his belly. His mouth opened in silent agony and he hit the dirty alley. I put the same shoe under his jaw and heard it break.

I walked away. Don't worry, boys. A cop will find you. You'll be taken to a hospital and the doctors will fix you right up, free of charge. Just send the bill to the decent, law-abiding, overburdened taxpayers of America . . . who can't afford health insurance.

I got the hell away from there, walking at a leisurely pace. Two blocks away, on a well-lighted street, I hailed a passing taxi and had him take me to a hotel far away from where I was registered. There, I had a drink in the bar and then got another taxi back to my hotel.

I washed my hands in the men's room and went to the dining room. The fish was delicious, the wine superb, and all in all, I felt marvelous. I had done the city of Portland a favor that night and they didn't even have to pay a cop overtime.

 Seven

I got back in Pine Hills just two days before my birthday. Checking in at the office, I chatted with Vic for almost an hour, bringing him up-to-date. Vic told everybody he didn't like to read reports, but I knew that was a sham to see who would slow down in the field and stop writing them. Vic Goodman read every word. After I'd briefed him, I told him I was tired and would like some time off.

He practically pounced on me. "Take as much time as you like, Larry-boy. My God, you been on the road at a flat lope for damn near a month. And knowin' you, you didn't even take time off to get laid."

I knew then that the field reps had gotten word to him of my refusing their offers of women. They were supposed to be sales reps, not procurement agents for the boss. But I felt no anger; they had only been doing what other bosses had expected of them in the past.

"What is today?" Vic asked, glancing at a calendar. "Thursday? I don't want to see you in this office 'til next

Thursday." He smiled hugely, pleased with himself for being so magnanimous. I figured roughly I had made him about five million dollars more than last year. "Git on outta here, boy. You have yourself a good time. Relax some."

I thanked him and got the hell out of there, leaving the fat fart grinning like a fool, waggling his fingers bye-bye at me. I disliked Vic more each time I saw him. I had soon realized there was no future for me with the Goodman Company, so I would salt away as much as possible, and then split. I had my eyes on a small company up in Missouri. It was in some trouble, and in about six months or so, I'd be able to buy it.

At the company-owned house, I called Tom Vanderwedge.

I had spoken with him three times in as many weeks. He had told me the country house was all mine—I just had to come by and sign the papers. He'd take care of the rest. The lights were turned on, the carpenters had finished, the phone was installed, the butane tank was filled, and a cord of firewood was stacked beside the house.

Tom was usually a very cheerful fellow, but he didn't sound so happy. I went by his office to pick up the keys, sign the papers, and chat with him for a time.

"You sure you remember the way out there?" he asked. But something was slightly out of whack with the way he phrased the question. Picking up on vocal nuances goes with the territory.

"Oh, sure," I replied, looking at him carefully. Something was very wrong with Tom's manner, his eyes a bit flat and unfriendly. "Tom, what's bothering you?"

He glared at me, anger now very much evident in his gaze. "You don't know?"

I hate questions like that. I'm not a mind reader. "Tom, I don't have any idea what you're talking about. I've been on the road for nearly a month. I've only been back in town slightly over three hours. Now, maybe you'd like to tell me about this big mystery that's got you all pissed off?"

He relaxed just a bit, some of the stiffness leaving his bearing. He nodded his head slowly. "I'm not behaving very professionally, I agree. It's Andy Mason."

"Andy Mason?" I had to think for a few seconds. Then it came to me.

"The young man Cody's been seeing," Tom prompted.

"Right. I remember now. Took me a few seconds to pull the name up. What about him?"

"He was attacked. Some thugs beat him up, that's what!" Tom blurted, obviously furious. But about what, I could not begin to fathom.

Leaning back in the chair, I said, "Well, Tom . . . that's too bad. I mean . . . I'm sorry for Cody and the boy, too, of course. I didn't know him. Only met him once, briefly. Exactly what did happen?" I wasn't all that broken up about it, but Cody had told me he was really a pretty nice guy and basically shy. They were friends and no more.

"Some punks jumped him in Atlanta about ten days ago. He had gone up there to escort Cody around. She was staying at the YW, he was at the YM."

The weekend I had called.

"It wasn't a mugging. Nothing was taken, nothing at all. What it amounted to was a systematic, thorough, professional-type beating. They knew what they were doing and they worked him over."

I still could not figure out why he was so upset with me. "How is he?"

"Oh, he'll live. He's up and walking around. Be able to return to work in about a week or so. But he was damn lucky, Larry. Really lucky. He could have been crippled or killed."

"How is Cody taking it?"

"She was upset. You haven't been in touch with her?"

"No, Tom. I haven't."

He stared at me.

I still didn't know why he was being so cold to me. I rose from the chair swiftly, loosening my tie.

Tom's face stiffened and he tensed.

"What the hell is wrong with you, Tom?"

"Nothing, really. I'm just curious as to why anyone would hire people to beat up a nice boy like Andy Mason."

"Well, hell, Tom! I don't know! Besides, how do the police know it was a hired beating? Maybe it was racial. Maybe it was gang motivated." I was beginning to get a little pissed as I stood over his desk, glaring at him.

"Sure, Larry."

"All right, Tom. Give." I sat back down. "What's the problem here? Something really stinks and I don't believe it's me."

He tried a thin smile that didn't make it past his lips. "All right, Larry. They train you boys pretty good in the Green Berets, don't they?"

"A green beret is headgear, Tom."

He waved that off. "They teach you people to kill, right?"

"That's correct, Tom. In all sorts of ways. From a piece of wire to a crossbow. Tom, will you please get to the point of all this? If there is any."

"I've heard some talk about ex-special forces people turning mercenary."

"Sure. So have I. And also some ex-priests, ex-school teachers, ex-CPA's, and people from nearly all walks of life. So what has any of this to do with me?"

"If I wanted someone beaten up, Larry, could you arrange it?"

Then I got his drift. I'd been thinking one way and he'd been taking a mental tack that had never dawned on me. Then I knew the reason he'd tensed up a few moments ago. I wasn't angry. Just disappointed. I put a level gaze on him and held it for about ten seconds. "Tom, are you nuts?"

He met my eyes and didn't back off. "Could you arrange to have someone beaten up, Larry?"

"Tom, if you're thinking I had anything to do with the Mason boy's beating, you're wrong. Flat-out wrong. Just about as far off base as you can get. I don't even know why you'd think such a thing."

"Because of all you've done and want to do for Cody. You can see where I might get ideas, can't you? It was pretty far out of character."

"I suppose so, Tom. But this damn sure doesn't say much for your opinion of me, now, does it?"

He sat and stared at me, as if seeing me for the first time. Maybe he was. "Larry, I wouldn't blame you if you took your business elsewhere."

"Is that what you want, Tom?"

"No. But don't expect me to apologize for what I was thinking."

"Then don't sweat it. Hell, you're the cheapest lawyer in town." I stood up, winked at him, and left.

I had a hide like an alligator.

Back then.

Before Cody.

"Cody? Larry. What are you doing later on this evening?"

She sounded just a bit subdued, but also genuinely glad to hear my voice. "I . . . ah . . . why, nothing, sir. Nothing at all."

"That's good, Cody. All us elders like respect from the young. *Sir.* That's very good."

"Yes, sir. And, sir? In about seven hours we can get it all settled, if that's all right with you. Sir," she added.

She was quick, giving me a code. I glanced at my watch. Seven hours would be seven-thirty. I had all afternoon to get ready. "Cody, look, I bought a place out by the creek. The old Norris house. Do you know where it is?"

"I certainly do, sir. And I certainly will, sir. Even though, as I am sure you're well aware, it's still two days early."

My birthday. She remembered. A warm, sort of unsettling glow filled me. I didn't know whether I liked that or not. I decided I did. "Well then, if you don't mind, try to keep Saturday open, too."

Only a second's hesitation. "Why . . . yes, sir. That would be fine. If you don't mind."

"I would like nothing better. I'll see you around seven-thirty, then."

"Yes, sir. And, sir? I'm glad you called. I've . . . been thinking about our last conversation."

"Me, too. See you, Cody."

"Yes, sir."

I had some things to do. I paused in the hallway, realizing I was behaving like a love-struck teenager.

Love! That brought me up short. I chuckled. That was absurd. Laughable. I just wanted to make it with the young lady, that's all.

My life, and certainly hers, would have been infinitely simpler had I just left it at that point. Made out, sure, then gotten off the bus. Parked the car, so to speak. But I had no way of knowing that Larry Baldwin was heading for the greatest and hardest fall of his life.

I bought a case of that horrid beer she liked, also a case of that equally abysmal wine. My small bar was well-stocked. The freezer was filled with steaks and other assorted goodies.

I looked at my watch. It was exactly five minutes later than the last time I'd looked.

I headed for a shopping mall just outside Atlanta. I wanted this weekend to be as right as I could possibly make it. I knew better than to push Cody; she was far too quick for that. So I would make it so pleasant out at the country house, so . . . right, with everything to her liking, she wouldn't need any urging from me. She would come there because she felt comfortable and wanted to. Eventually, I'd make it with her. Because I always get my way. This time would be no different. Not at all.

Veni, Vidi, Vici.

Yeah. Right.

During a previous trip to this mall, I had purchased a compact but very expensive stereo system, complete with enough speaker power to stun the fish in the creek behind the house. Now, I steeled myself for the ordeal ahead: I went into a record shop that was playing the most godawful music I have ever heard.

About the only thing my father had done constructively in his entire life was to instill in me a deep appreciation for classical music. I had not kept up with music trends since high school, and once inside the shop, I was grateful I hadn't.

The young man behind the counter seemed to be in some sort of trance. He had a difficult time getting his eyes to focus on me. I finally got his attention by holding up a hundred-dollar bill and waving it in front of him. Over the roar of the music, I asked, "That . . . song playing—is it popular?"

"Oh, my, sir. Yes. That's number one on the charts."

"I see," I said, looking at him for a moment. He was bobbing up and down. "Why is it number one?"

My question jarred him out of his mystical ponderings. "I beg your pardon, sir?"

"Forget it. Look, I'm buying some albums for a friend. Her birthday. She'll be twenty-two. And as far as I can tell, she's . . . ah, what's the word? *Cool* was in when I was a kid."

He smiled sadly. By all means, patronize the old dude. He probably ain't got long to go. Must be at least forty. Maybe forty-five. "I know exactly what you want, sir." He held up a CD. "This is what is playing. You really want something in this vein."

The front cover startled me. Twenty-five years ago, possession of just the cover would have been grounds for imprisonment. I stared at it in disbelief. And at the name of the group. "What in God's name is a Sucked Duck?"

The young man looked hurt. "It's a group, sir."

"A group of what?"

"Sir?"

"Never mind. I see. I think."

"The Sucked Duck is backed on this session by the Bowel Movement," he informed me.

I really could have done without that information. "You have to be kidding!"

"Oh, no, sir. Really. All the critics say they certainly have it all together."

"Is it contagious?"

"Sir?"

"Never mind. All right. Whatever you say." He had been helpful and I had no right to put down his music. But five will get you ten he would have put down mine. "You pick out the CDs."

"Very good, sir. How many? Four, five?"

"Fifty."

He paled. *"Fifty?"*

"Yes. What's the matter, are you ill?" If he wasn't he soon would be, listening to that racket pouring from the speakers. I had noticed that the older shoppers almost always avoided walking directly in front of the record shop.

"Oh, no, sir." He bobbed and weaved off, in high heel semi-Western boots.

I'll give him credit—he didn't just jerk and grab to please the old dude and get him out of his shop. He carefully selected each CD, consulting some sort of chart several times. Then he got sweaty totaling up the bill.

He was hesitant in announcing the sum. "Fine," I told him, and handed him a credit card.

I drove back to the house with the radio tuned to various Atlanta rock stations. I wanted to see if all the rock and roll was as bad as the stuff I'd endured back at the record shop. Some of it was, some wasn't.

I had killed several hours driving to the city, shopping, and then returning to my new place. I had seen no one I knew, coming or going. Two and a half hours before jump-off time. It was dark out. I tried the outside light. It worked. I did a careful walk-through of the house, inspecting the recent work. The carpenters had done a good job. There were a few areas that still needed work, but I wanted Cody to see the house and offer her opinion as to what might go where, give her a feeling of belonging. Let her pick out new drapes and carpet, some furniture, if that's what she wanted. By the end of spring, or at the latest, early summer, I'd be gone and Tom could sell the damn house.

I had it all worked out, battle plan carefully laid out in segments—subject to last-minute revision, of course. Again, I paced through the house, pausing to add another log to the fire. I stepped out onto the porch. The temperature was falling rapidly. Everything checked out A-okay. It was as good as I could make it.

I showered, shaved, dressed, thanks to Norm Thompson and L.L. Bean, then slipped my feet into loafers and fixed a light drink of Crown Royal and water.

I watched the flames and waited for Cody.

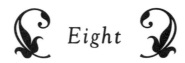 *Eight*

"I love it," Cody said, looking around the house. "I sure like it a whole lot better than that place you have in town. And the neighbors are nicer, too."

I smiled at that. "I don't have any neighbors out here, Cody."

"That's what I mean."

She spied the new stereo and laughed in delight, moving over to the rack that held the CDs, still encased in cellophane. She fingered through the discs, saying nothing. The expression on her face amused me.

She was like a rainbow after the storm, dressed in a purple shirt and blue jeans. The reflection of the flames from the fireplace danced in her glossy black hair. As she leaned over the stereo, I could not help but admire her denim-clad rump. A very shapely derriere indeed. I still did not understand my feelings toward her as I mentally slipped the jeans from her. I was after one thing and nothing would have convinced me otherwise. The adage that there is no fool like an old fool did not apply to me.

She turned, shards of light from the fire licking around her, highlighting the midnight of her hair, burnishing her skin, creating little pockets of mystery in the shadows of her curves.

"I didn't know you liked this kind of music, Larry," she said.

"I don't, particularly. But I thought you might like some of this."

She waved at the CDs and the stereo set. "All this must have cost a lot of money, Larry."

I shrugged. "So I'll write it off as entertainment expense."

She looked at me strangely as she opened one CD. "And who pays for that in the long run, Larry?"

"What do you mean?"

"You know what I mean. The consumers who buy your products eventually pay for it, don't they?"

"I . . . guess that's one way of looking at it." I knew she was right, of course.

She stood staring at me. "That's the only way to look at it. One of these days, Larry, if prices keep going up and up, the bottom is going to fall out of our economy and a lot of people are going to get hurt."

"You're a very astute young lady."

"I watch the evening news. I read the newspapers. Big-shot CEOs and presidents of companies and corporations making millions and millions. Nobody is worth that kind of money."

"Tell that to high-priced athletes."

"They're sure as hell not worth it. But if the fans are stupid enough to let ticket prices skyrocket, then it's their own fault."

"How about paying a hundred bucks to see some rock group, Cody?"

"I wouldn't pay a hundred bucks to see the reincarnation of Elvis." She slipped the CD into the slide-out rack on the stereo and turned the volume down low. "I'll break you in gently, Larry," she said with a smile.

Nice choice of words, I thought. I have exactly the same plans for you, dear.

Turned down low, the music wasn't all that bad. Heavy on bass and drums, with, I suppose, muted overtones of primitive sex. The lyrics were incomprehensible gruntings. I tuned them out and let the music drive through my head.

"You're a different person, Larry," Cody remarked, sitting down in a chair across the small den from me. And that was to be "Her Chair." Where I sat was to be "My Chair." "I've never seen you looking so . . . *rustic*, I guess is the word."

I smiled across the fire-lit expanse. "You know how it is, Cody, big-shot executives have to dress the part. But that doesn't mean that we can't relax with friends in our spare time." Nice speech, Larry. You remembered it word for word. Now let's see if the lady bought the *friend* bit.

Her eyes were like pale fingers searching my face. "And *are* we friends, Larry?"

"Of course."

"Someone I can tell my troubles to? Be at ease with? All that goes with having a friend?"

I wondered if she was really that naive. Or just lonely. I didn't think Cody was naive, so I settled on lonely. "That's me, Cody. I'll always be right here when you need someone to talk to or lean on."

"Why, Larry? Why . . . you and me?"

She was definitely suspicious. I lifted my hands in a gesture of "who knows?" "Why don't we just call it . . . hell, I don't know. Fate, perhaps."

She looked at me for several seconds, then smiled oddly. I didn't—at the time—know whether she bought that verbal crap or not. But she nodded her head affirmatively. "Do you have anything to drink in this house?"

"I laid in a small stock. Look in the refrigerator and the cabinet beside it."

She did and her laughter rang through the small house. "Larry! God, you've got enough booze in here for half the town. Just look at all this stuff. Hey! What's in this container here, this funny-looking, icky stuff?"

I laughed at her description of marinade. "Steaks, Cody. They're marinating. I thought you might like something to eat after a time. I'll light the charcoal whenever you're ready."

She opened the lid and looked inside. "God, Larry. Those aren't steaks. That's half the cow!"

"When I want a steak, I want a steak. How do you like yours cooked?"

"I don't have steaks very often. But when I do, I like them rare."

"Good girl. So do I."

She returned to her chair with a chilled bottle of that horrible wine. She was silent for a moment, her face a study, then got out of the chair to sit cross-legged on the floor in front of me, drinking the wine straight out of the bottle. She looked up and tried a smile that did not come across.

I thought I knew the reason for her sadness and took a stab at it. "I was sorry to hear about your boyfriend, Cody."

"Thanks. But he isn't my boyfriend. We were just good friends, that's all. We were going to a concert, later on. I warned Andy not to walk, but he just laughed at me. Kind of like you did that night. But Andy isn't nearly as rough as you. I don't think he ever had a fight in his whole entire life. Oh, you know, grade school stuff, that's all. His size usually kept him out of fights."

"You think I'm that rough, Cody?"

"Yes. I do. You are. I just know. Your eyes never give away very much, and you're in control, all the time. Most men your age have the beginnings of a big beer belly, but you're solid like a rock. You move like a big cat. I think you're a very dangerous man, Larry Baldwin. But you keep it under control. I think you're a predator, Larry. But a nice one."

Predator, yes. Nice? I'd been called a lot of things in my life. *Nice* had never been one of them.

"What caused the fight, Cody?"

"I really don't know and neither does Andy. He was walking over to get me. He thinks it was some sort of gang initiation—all teenagers, he said."

"He was lucky they didn't shoot him."

"Andy says he's leaving this area." Cody slugged back some wine. "Says he's been wanting to get away for a year and this was all the excuse he needed."

"Where's he going?"

"Down around Macon. He has an uncle down there who offered him a job in construction. There's nothing around here, unless you want to work for lard-butt Goodman. And since Andy is a friend of mine, Vic put the word out on him, too."

Her mood shifted and she smiled up at me. "I have a birthday present for you, Larry. But I'm not going to give it to you until Saturday."

I returned the smile. "Now that's not fair, Cody. You're keeping me in suspense."

She shook her head and took another swallow. "Nope. Saturday."

"Well," I said, waving at the stereo and the CDs. "You may consider this as your present. But I may pick you up a little bauble as a surprise."

"You already did, Larry," she said quietly, those pale eyes on my face.

"Oh? What's that?" I didn't have any idea what she was talking about.

"That Toyota parked in the drive. One day I can't get financing, the next day I can. I stopped believing in Santa Claus a long time ago, Larry. Come on, 'fess up."

I shook my head. "Okay, okay. Damn, girl! How do you do these things? Are you some sort of psychic?"

"No. But I'm pretty good at figuring things out."

I should have known right then and there she knew exactly what I was up to.

"Now you tell me who I'm making the payments to, Larry. Is it you?"

I said nothing, thinking fast. If I wasn't careful, the evening would quickly turn into a total ruin. I had been warned about Care packages.

"Don't lie to me, Larry," she whispered, her words just audible over the pulsing of the rock music pushing softly from the speakers.

I honest-to-God had never wanted to kiss a pair of lips so badly in all my life.

"All right." My voice was just loud enough for her to hear. "I won't lie to you. In a roundabout way you're paying me. But you had to have some way to get to work. Your job is too far away to walk. Dammit, I was just trying to help you, that's all." Lie, Larry. Lie convincingly or you'll blow it. Then all your plans will go right out the window and into the cold. And you'll be stuck with this stupid house miles from nowhere.

I rose swiftly from the chair, a habit of mine when I'm trying to think quickly, or have a lot on my mind. And I can move very quickly. I saw Cody flinch at the movement.

She's afraid of me, I thought. The girl is physically afraid of me. That angered me. "Why did you flinch?" I towered over her, my voice harder than I intended.

She blinked up at me. "You . . . startled me, that's all. You move very well for a man . . ." She cut that short.

"For a man forty years old," I finished it.

She shrugged her shoulders.

"I'm a long way from being over the hill, Cody."

"I didn't say you were over the hill. I can see that you're not. Please don't spoil this evening, Larry. I don't want it spoiled. For you or me."

My quick spurt of anger was gone as swiftly as it came. But there was still a hint of harshness left in my voice. "Why, Cody? Is tonight special to you?"

Those beautiful eyes touched me. "Yes, it is, Larry. For

some . . . reason, I like you. I want to trust you. But I get this feeling, somehow, that you aren't being—and this is going to make you mad—totally honest with me."

"But I am being honest with you, Cody." Something shifted deep within me at the lie. It was almost a physical pain.

She looked up at me for a moment. "All right, Larry." But her tone had a flatness to it.

She was going to take just a bit more convincing and I knew just the line. "Now, Cody, it's my turn. I can sense that you don't believe me. But answer this: why would I lie? What reason would I have? Lusting after your young body?" I laughed at that and her eyes darkened with fire.

Everything was working out just fine. I knew that last remark would create a spark. I've used it before. It works most of the time.

The female in her leaped to the surface. "You don't find me attractive?"

"Yes, I do, Cody. Of course I do." That was my most honest statement of the evening—so far. "I find you very attractive. And just saying that is an understatement. Believe me, it is."

I walked over to the small bar in the den and watched her rise from the floor effortlessly. She walked over to stand by me. She put her hand on my arm and the warmth from that small hand was like a branding iron. Again, that shifting sensation from deep within me touched a part of me that I thought I had locked away years back. But something began tugging, rattling the bars around my long-barricaded emotions.

"Cody, I know the past couple of weeks must have been

tough. But today has been trying for me, too. That's why I'm a little uptight. Tom Vanderwedge accused me of having Andy beat up. I didn't like that."

Her eyes widened and her lips formed an O.

"Yeah." I picked up her shock. "Me, too. I just sat there and stared at him. I just could not believe what he was saying."

"Oh, Larry," she whispered, taking a half-step closer. She was awfully close. Close enough for me to smell her body heat. The female scent pounded me in a sensual rhythm, arousing me. "I'm so sorry he said that." She never took her eyes from mine. I got the feeling she was trying to see into my soul. Maybe she was. Maybe she did. Maybe she thought there was some hope left for me. "But Mr. Vanderwedge has known me since I was born. He's just concerned, that's all."

"I know. I know. But . . . it bothered me. Cody, I never had a young friend. As an adult, that is. Never could get close to a young person. My fault, I suppose. Never met a young person quite like you." Never wanted to screw someone so badly in all my life.

She put a soft hand on my cheek and I just about lost my carefully maintained cool. "I like you, Larry," she said, her eyes searching my face like radar. "I've been hurt before, and I've taken a lot of crap from the so-called 'good people' of this community. I . . . I just don't want to be hurt anymore, that's all. And I don't want you to think we have something that we really don't."

"I don't think that at all, Cody." I touched her cheek with a fingertip and sensed that was as far as I'd better travel this time around. I smiled down at her. "Friends?"

She kissed me on the cheek like a trusting child. "Yes, Larry. We're friends."

The evening was perfect after that. She got into the wine pretty good and got the giggles after I reached into the fridge for the steaks and dropped the whole damn mess on the kitchen floor. Marinade went flying all over the place and the steaks looked like something out of a science-fiction movie as they lay on the floor.

"The Blob," I said.

"The what?" she asked, helping me find a mop and a handful of paper towels.

I spent the next several minutes telling her about Steve McQueen's early movie. I started to toss the steaks into the garbage and she set up a howl of protest.

"Don't waste good meat!" She took the steaks and washed them off under the faucet, plopped them on a plate, and pushed me toward the back door with orders to cook; she'd see about the potatoes and the salad. Cook, Larry!

It was then I began to feel just a tiny, tiny bit of guilt at what I had planned for Cody. That strange sensation once more began to move around in me, upsetting all my carefully made schemes. The evening, after our brief moment of tension, had again begun to level out. It was right. I felt good. It was as if something had suddenly jelled between us; a bond had been set.

And after all I put her through in the few months that lay ahead of us, I realize it was that night that it all really started.

Standing on the back porch, feeling the cold winds mix with the heat from the charcoal, I looked at her through the kitchen window and felt something good and decent touch me. I didn't know what to do with the feeling; I had never experienced anything quite like it. The sensation was so alien to me, so strange . . . I rudely pushed away the tenderness it brought and centered all my thoughts on getting this one particular young lady into my bed. But try though I did, the feeling would not entirely leave me.

I refused to allow the conflict within me to put a damper on the evening. I helped Cody in the kitchen, laughing and kidding with her about how she could do the dishes after dinner.

"*We'll* do the dishes," she corrected. "You and me. You and I. Whatever. Us."

We ate in the den, on TV trays. She had put on a CD that seemed to pretty well fit the mood. I suppose it was her generation's answer to Nat King Cole. But the guy had a hell of a long way to go before ever jeopardizing the King's reputation.

"Like it?" Cody asked.

"The music?"

She nodded, her mouth too full of rib eye to speak.

"Yes. In a way. And that surprises me."

She smiled. "You see? My age group is not all bad, are we?"

"No," I offered softly. "No, definitely not, Cody."

She stared at me for a long moment, then grinned and turned her attention to the steak.

We did the dishes, or rather, rinsed them off before sticking them in the dishwasher. I felt a certain peace within me, with her, while we did those simple things. Cody caught me looking at her and paused there by the sink, smiling.

"What are you thinking, Larry Baldwin?"

I knew I'd damn well better level with her, and I did. "I was thinking how much I like you, Cody. And . . . some other thoughts, as well." I did not elaborate on those other thoughts. I really had not meant to say it. Damn honesty, anyway!

We walked into the den and took up positions in Our Chairs.

"What other things, Larry?"

Think fast, Baldwin. Real fast. Hey, now! Why not try honesty for a change? Maybe that's the tack you should have taken all along. I rejected that immediately but decided to level with her, in part. "You've known me—been alone with me—a total of what, Cody? Ten or twelve hours at the max? Yet here you are, with me, almost a stranger, in my house, stuck 'way out in the country. We're alone. No neighbors. That . . . confuses me. I'll admit that. It does. And I don't like that feeling. Are you always this trusting?"

"You won't hurt me, Larry. I'm . . . well, I'm a little bit afraid of you—if that's the right choice of words, and it probably isn't. But I know, sense, that you're not the type to force yourself on women. You don't have to, and probably never had to. A lot of women are attracted to men like you. You might . . . try something with me, sometime. I expect you will. You're a man. But you're also my friend, and that will stop you."

Jesus! The kid could really hit below the belt. What a load she was dumping on me. All I could do was nod in agreement. "You, ah, often go to peoples' houses, Cody? I mean, people you don't know very well?"

"Almost never. Most people in Pine Hills wouldn't have me in their homes. I'm white trash, Larry, or hasn't Vic Goodman told you that?"

"You can knock that off, Cody. You're no more white trash than I am."

"And just how do you know that, Larry?"

"I just do."

"The same way I know you won't hurt me?"

I smiled. "Yeah, Cody. I guess. The same way."

She returned the smile. But hers was genuine, filled with trust and honesty. "I have two places in Pine Hills that I go. Friends' homes. You know, we drink some wine, play guitars—they play, I have a tin ear. We just talk about things."

We were silent for a time. She broke the silence by asking, "Where do you go when you want to talk something out, Larry?"

I shook my head. "No place. Talk to myself."

"That's no good. You can talk to me from now on."

"I . . . think I'd like that. Yeah, I would. But you might get bored."

"Well, we'll just have to see, won't we?"

Then we lost track of time as we talked of many things. The hours hurtled by unchecked. I glanced at my watch and was shocked to see it was almost two o'clock in the morning. I could not remember ever having enjoyed myself so much.

"Hey, Cody. You have to work today, remember?"

"What time is it?"

I had never seen her wear a watch, wondered if she even owned one. "Two o'clock."

She sighed. "I don't remember ever having so much fun. The time really went by, didn't it?"

"Yes, it did." I found her jacket and slipped it over her shoulders. I made no move to touch her. On the porch, in the freezing air of Georgia winter, she turned and kissed me. I slipped my arms around her and returned the kiss, then carefully released her.

She looked up at me, surprise in her eyes. She cocked her head to one side, waiting for me to do what else I might have in mind.

"See you Saturday night, Cody."

She nodded and smiled, then laughed, and was gone, running to her car. She paused for a second, waved, and then jumped in and was gone, driving too fast, naturally.

I stood on the porch for several minutes, long past the moment her taillights had faded into the night. Leaning against the porch railing, I touched my fingertips to my lips. The scent of her was on my mouth, my shirt, my hands, and the feel of her was still alive all around me. I didn't know, didn't understand, what was happening to me. This just wasn't working out the way I'd so carefully planned it.

But I had to admit I rather liked the warm glow.

 *Nine*

I did not leave the house all day Friday, except for a couple of short strolls around the property and down along the creek that ran behind the house. I was content, and that contentment came as a real surprise. I was happy to sit quietly reading, or listening to music—some of the rock CDs I'd bought for Cody, and some of the classics I'd bought for myself—or just dozing in the big, overstuffed chair. My chair. Which faced her chair. Which was empty.

Saturday was the longest day I had ever spent. I cleaned the house, from top to bottom, mopping the floors, vacuuming the carpet, and every five minutes glancing at the clock. I expected Cody to call. She did not. It was full dark at five o'clock and turning very cold, but the fireplace was merry with flames, dancing out heat to the beat of crackling wood.

My fear and suspicion were confirmed: Cody did not make her promised appearance that night. My disappointment was overshadowed only by my growing anger and resentment.

"Resentment?" I said aloud. Then I laughed. But the laughter was void of humor.

Resentment at what—at whom? Cody? Why? What did you expect from someone half your age, with a totally different set of values? Come on, Larry! Shape up, boy. What the hell? So you lost this game. Big deal.

"I don't like to lose," I muttered.

I paced the floor and tried to think it out. Finally, I settled on what I thought was fact: she was with her own age group, sitting at a friend's house, listening to Heavy Metal and getting high on that terrible wine.

And giving no thought to you, you big, stupid, conceited bastard. None at all. No doubt laughing to herself about it. Or worse, telling her friends about this old dude who was trying to put the hustle on her. And here you are, you big dummy, you high-priced, top-level executive type, a so-called adult and self-made man, pacing the floor and behaving like some love-struck adolescent.

God, Larry, you're pathetic. It's your turn to grow up, boy.

But all the time I was wishing the phone would ring and it would be Cody, telling me she was on the way out to see me.

But the phone did not ring.

I fixed a martini and lifted the glass in a toast to Cody. "You saw through my game, set me up, and knocked the pins right out from under me, kid. Good play. You outfoxed the hunter. I give you credit for staying one jump ahead of me the whole time."

I sat in My Chair and drank martinis. By the time I fixed supper and went to bed, I had a pretty good buzz going, and thinking some very mixed thoughts about a certain young lady. Love and hate. Anger and sorrow. Pity and condemnation. All the emotions directed at . . .

Thank you for visiting the
Allen County Public Library.

Item ID: 31833041728988
Title: What the heart knows
: a love story
Author: Johnstone, William
W.
Date due: 1/24/2012,23:59

Telephone Renewal: 421-
1240
Website Renewal: www.acpl.
info

Cody or myself?

I wasn't too sure about that.

One thing I'm sure of is that it would have been much better for the both of us had she come out then. I would have unloaded on her and whatever we had going would have ended right there. Yes, it would have been much better for all concerned.

But if it had, then I would never have learned what my heart had been trying to tell me all along.

Sunday morning, after taking some aspirin in an attempt to soothe a slight hangover, I buttoned up the country house and drove back to town, to the company house.

On the drive in, I muttered, "Happy birthday, Larry. And do yourself a favor and stay the hell away from kids from now on, huh?"

But I could not get Cody out of my mind.

Vic was surprised when I strolled into his office Monday morning.

"Boy?" he said, leaning back in his custom-made chair and looking at me. "What the hell are you doin' back here? I thought I told you not to come back 'til Thursday." He rose and stuck out his hand.

I shook the hand and said, "That long weekend did the trick, Vic. It was exactly what I needed. Now I want to get back to work, get cracking. I need to fly down to Mobile and straighten out that sloppy office there." And work off some of the lingering mad I still had at Cody, at being taken like a hick tourist.

"Whatever you say, Larry-boy."

"But," I said with a smile, "I may surprise you and take the remainder of those days off at a moment's notice. If you know what I mean?" I winked lewdly. Man-to-man wink.

"Oh, yeah!" He grinned, leaning back in his chair. "I get you. I'm right glad you got yourself a woman, boy. Hell, you got the vacation time comin'. Take it whenever you want it. Gettin' serious, hey, boy?"

"Might very well be, Vic. But it's still a little early to tell."

He laughed and pounded the desk. I left him howling and slapping his desk and pulling at his crotch. I disliked the man intensely. Perhaps it was because I had suddenly found more than a little bit of Victor Goodman in me. And that was disgusting.

I wondered if that newfound knowledge had anything to do with meeting Cody. Probably, I concluded.

I spent two days and nights in Mobile, shaping up our office in that lovely city and taking some of my fury out on the manager and his salespeople. For the first time since I'd had any power at all in this business—and that went back years—I created a scene in a manager's office. I did not like the man in charge and made no attempt to disguise those feelings. I left him with a warning that if he didn't shape up, the next time I came through the door, I would be carrying his walking papers. The hate he felt for me was only thinly veiled in his angry eyes. But what he felt for and about me did not concern me at all. The business world is tough, and if a person can't hack it, then get the hell out.

The manager and many of his staff would not last with the Goodman Company. I could sense that. Vic would not tolerate failure. But on the flight back to the small company-owned strip in Pine Hills, I didn't feel my usual euphoria after going in and pulling together a sloppy office. I felt drained, let down, depressed.

I could not get Cody out of my mind and that angered me, the chafing finally overriding the depression, leaving me in, to use one of Cody's expressions, a funk. I was surly with the pilot and had to fight back the urge to deck him when I turned my head and glimpsed the middle finger he saluted me with as I walked away from the plane. I ignored the rigid digit and headed for the office.

After I made my report to Vic, he stopped me as I got up to leave. "You and your little woman have a phone-fuss, Larry-boy? You in a foul mood."

"Something like that, Vic."

"They are aggravatin', ain't they?"

"At times, Vic. At times."

"Ain't it the truth?"

I was feeling much better by the time Friday evening crawled past the afternoon's dusk and pulled down the shades over Georgia. I had plans for dinner for one, sitting for a time by the fire with a brandy, and maybe listening to some old songs from the late forties and early fifties. Ol' Blue Eyes, maybe. I had picked up some "greatest hits" CDs of Frank and Tony and I looked forward to hearing them sing of lost love—"One For My Baby" and "Boulevard of Broken Dreams."

I really was not feeling maudlin, and I'm way too young to remember all the music of the late forties and early fifties— but nevertheless I like much of that music. The singers have something absolutely necessary: it's called talent.

I was sitting thinking about supper, the music drifting around me, when the knock on the front door halted my mental journey into the kitchen. It was a woman's knock, unlike a man's heavy hand. And I knew who it was.

I opened the door. "Hi, Larry." Cody smiled the words at me, a gaily wrapped package in one gloved hand. "I brought you your birthday present."

All the anger and resentment and frustration of the past week vanished without a trace. That dull ache began just under my heart, and that funny-odd-strange sensation began its meanderings inside me.

"Come on in, Cody." I stepped aside. The scent of her filled my head, drifting around me like a gentle, fragrant cloud. I would have to find out what kind of perfume she wore. It was just right for her. And for me. "Perfect timing, Cody. Just in time for dinner. You like lobster tail?"

"I don't know. I never had any."

"Well, we'll see."

She handed me the package. "Happy . . . belated birthday, Larry. Please open it."

I took her coat and hung it in the hall closet and then turned to let my eyes travel over her body as she walked to the fireplace. I had to smile. It's always easy to tell the difference between a city woman and a country woman. Works nearly all the time. A city woman will put her hands out to warm them on the open flames. A country girl will almost always stick her butt toward the fire.

My present was a gold money clip, and a damned expensive one, with a name engraved on it: FRIEND.

Oh, Cody, this is hitting below the belt.

"Do you like it, Larry?" she asked, both hands rubbing her rapidly heating, denim-clad rear.

"Yes, I do, Cody. I like it very much and I do need one. But I wish you hadn't done it. It's expensive and I know you need your money for other things."

She shrugged and smiled mysteriously. "So, what are you going to do? Repossess my car if I miss a payment?"

I stared at her for a moment, then laughed. "Sure, Cody. You know I'm going to do that."

Our eyes met. Locked. Held. Neither of us dropped the intense gaze. I have played that scene back in my mind hundreds of times. It's as vivid today as it was then. Something moved between us on that cold winter's night in the country. At the time, she knew what it was—I didn't. But my heart did. I just wasn't listening.

She broke the silence. "I'm sorry I didn't come back Saturday, Larry. I know I told you that I would. But . . . I just didn't know if I should."

"I don't understand that last bit. But I'm glad you came out tonight."

"Did you get mad at me for not coming out?"

"I will have to admit, I was a bit . . . displeased when you didn't keep your word."

She moved away from the fireplace and took a step in my direction. "Pissed off, you mean."

I smiled at her. "Yeah, Cody. Pissed off is the term, I suppose."

We continued to stare at one another, standing a few yards apart, neither of us saying anything. The grown man with a touch of gray at the temples, and the lovely young lady with the midnight hair and the fascinating pale eyes.

That strange force began its travels, touching each of us, almost electric in its movement. A spark seeking something to ignite.

"Thank you for my present, Cody."

"You're welcome, Larry."

Conversation didn't just lag after that—it died. Then that strange spark began darting back and forth as we continued to stare at each other. After a moment, Cody turned away to face the blazing fire.

I cleared my throat and shuffled my feet. "Well . . . I'd better get those lobster tails ready and see about some vegetables. You like vegetables, Cody?"

She turned around. I thought I could see tears in her eyes. "Oh, yes, everything except boiled okra." She blinked a couple of times. There *were* tears in her eyes. She tried a smile. "Can I help?"

"Fix the salad?"

"Sure."

Together, we walked into the small kitchen. It seemed that no matter how hard we tried not to, every time we turned around, we were bumping into each other, hands touching, hips bumping. She got the giggles and I felt wonderful.

After dinner, we took Our Chairs by the fire after I poured snifters of brandy. Cody took one sip, gagged, and flatly announced that was the shittiest stuff she had ever tasted. She started to toss it into the fire.

"No!" I yelled. "God, don't do that. It'll go off like lighter fluid."

She grimaced, running her tongue over her lips. She nodded in agreement. "This mess ought to explode. Tastes like gasoline. I'm gonna get some wine."

I started laughing, and it was a genuine, open laugh, the first time I'd laughed that openly since . . . well, the last time Cody had been here.

She returned with a bottle of chilled sweet wine, the kind you can buy on skid row and in little convenience stores, the latter being where I got the stuff.

"What's so funny, Larry?"

"You. I think you're a genuine, one-of-a-kind character, Cody."

"I guess." She plopped down in her chair. "A lot of people sure think that. My parents did, too. Even when I was little, I was always doing all sorts of off-the-wall things. I'm just me, that's all. I am what I was created to be, and I'm comfortable with it."

"Don't ever change, Cody."

She took a sip right out of the bottle and shifted her eyes to me. Her gaze was more than searching; it seemed to cut right through me. "Do you like the way I am, Larry?"

I came very close to saying: *I love the way you are*. I bit the words off before they could leave my lips. Love? Love! Oh, come on, Baldwin. Don't be ridiculous. You might be in heat, but you are not in love. Love? You don't know the meaning of the word. You just want to get the girl's pants off, that's all.

Isn't that all there is to it, Baldwin?

Isn't it?

Sure it is.

Okay. So that's settled.

"Yes, Cody. I like you just the way you are. I do very much like you."

"Okay." She tossed her head, the raven hair tumbling about her face. "Then I won't change. Just for you, Mister Big-Shot Larry Baldwin. Super-dooper salesman."

"And you do keep your word, right?" I asked drily.

She smiled. "When I want to."

We sat and talked for another hour or so. I sipped expensive brandy and she sipped supermarket wine straight out of the bottle. Just before she left, saying—promising, cross my heart and hope to die, Larry—that she would be back the next evening, we stood on the cold porch and she got up on tippy-toes and kissed me.

"About seven tomorrow evening?" I asked.

"On the dot, Larry."

There was a mysterious twinkle in her eyes that I could not read, and being the suspicious type, it bothered me. "What are you up to, Cody?"

She was standing very close to me, her breasts lightly pushing against my chest. She looked up at me. "Why . . . whatever in the world do you mean?"

That twinkle was still very much in her eyes. "Something is going on with you, Cody. I'm picking up some strange signals. Vibes, you might call them."

"Oh? Naw. Not from me. It's just your imagination working overtime, Larry." She kissed me again and said, "Bye, now." She went skipping to her car, waved at me, and was gone in the night. She drove entirely too fast.

I stood on the porch and watched the car disappear into the distance.

I slept better that night than I had in a week, at first dreaming nice, gentle dreams of a petite young lady with dark hair and pale blue eyes.

But then the dream changed, turning strangely ominous and murky. It was night, but oddly lighted with flashes of different colors. People were running and yelling, saying things I could not understand. Vic Goodman was there, laughing and holding something, someone; I couldn't see clearly enough to determine just what it was he was hanging onto.

I was in a panic. I knew that for a fact. But over what?

Then the dream began to fade. First the lights dimmed into nothing, then the shapes of people running about began to evaporate; the yelling and screaming hushed, and Vic Goodman vanished.

I dreamed of Cody once more and all was well.

 *Ten*

I awakened early and refreshed. I had forgotten all about the strange dream. I made coffee and clicked on the television. The TV weather lady said that two fronts were about to do something and when they did whatever it was they were about to do, it was going to give us a lot of rain, beginning about Saturday midmorning, then change to sleet and snow and freezing rain by late afternoon or early evening. I hoped the lady was wrong, for I did not want anything to interfere with Cody's visit.

It began to rain about nine o'clock that morning, at first only a slight drizzle, the sky sullen-looking with ominous clouds. Then the temperature began falling, rapidly. One did not have to be a weather lady to know what that meant: snow.

Just about two o'clock I stood on the front porch and watched as the first bits of sleet and snow fell from the sky. Crap! No way Cody would be coming out here with all this glop falling, and I hoped she wouldn't risk it.

Now, looking back, I wished she had not come. Things would have been so different for both of us, had just one of us elected to stay on the safe side, and that person should have been me. I was the so-called adult. I should have called Cody and told her not to come. But I blew it. Fate is a quirky lady, handing out great happiness one moment, then ripping it away the next.

I sat in the den that snowy day and thought about Cody and my feelings for her. I reviewed each time we'd met, and they were few. But they were also somehow strangely precious.

On that sleety-snowy afternoon, I slipped mentally back in time, back to every girl I might have ever been serious with in high school and college. And I found there were none. I reviewed my adult life and found the same emotional void. At no time that I could recall, in any relationship, including my marriage, had my feelings matched the affection I felt for Cody.

Then . . . what was happening to me? What the hell was this . . . this passion?

That afternoon I had first seen Cody on the street, coming out of that dress shop, I had thought, and I recalled it vividly, that I liked her style. Then, a few months later, in that rock joint in Atlanta, I had felt something odd well up in me. Then that clumsy attempt to help her get into a school. Had I done that solely to get into her pants? I sighed. No, I didn't believe so. A five-thousand-dollar brief fling? No. Financing a car for her? Add some more thousands to the total. No. No. That wasn't Baldwin's style at all. Baldwin is much too frugal for anything like that. Until lately, that is. Bailing her out of jail at the risk of losing everything I'd worked for? Again, not my style. Nothing I had done thus far was my style. It was all out of character. Everything.

I sat in the den for a long time that wintry afternoon, deep in thought as the storm worsened and the snow piled up outside the snug country home, the only sounds the crackling from the fireplace, the faint popping as sleet pelted the windows, and the ever-searching wind.

I rose from the chair and walked around the den, muttering and shaking my head. I paused at a front window. Snow was coming down in white, whirling, nearly blinding sheets, and amid the glistening diamonds, all mixed in with the paleness, were bits of sleet and freezing rain. The snow was so thick it was lightening the evening sky. This was indeed a rare event in Central Georgia.

I put another log on the fire, stoked it up, then went to the bar and fixed a drink and returned to stand by the window.

I stared out at the road. It looked slick and dangerous. "Don't try it, Cody," I muttered. "Stay home with your aunt and be safe."

I lifted my eyes and looked up the road as a pair of headlights cut their way into the drive.

Cody.

I stepped onto the porch just as she got out of the Toyota, a bottle of that horrible wine in one hand. She laughed and waved and shouted at me.

"Hey, Larry-Big-Shot!" She waved the bottle at me. I could see that she was well on her way to getting juiced. "I told you I'd come see you, didn't I?"

"Cody, you little fool!" I yelled, then rushed off the porch toward her. Bad mistake on my part. I hit the steps and felt my feet fly out from under me as they touched the ice on the bottom step. I managed to get off the steps and onto the ground before I started doing a little circus act, but still went down, busting my butt in the snow. The glass in my hand went sailing away. Getting cautiously to my feet, I flailed and slipped, waving my arms for balance. Cody was doubled over, laughing hysterically. I hit the snow-covered ground again as my feet slipped out from under me. Cody was laughing so hard she had to lean against her car for support. I had never seen her laugh like that before. I couldn't help but grin at myself. That's one thing I can do, despite all my other faults—I can laugh at myself.

Getting to my feet again, I made my way cautiously toward her. "Dammit, Cody!" I bellowed. "The roads are treacherous." Then, before I realized what I was doing, I had my arms around her and she had her arms around me. With the steam from our breath smoking the cold air, I said, "You could have been killed or hurt, Cody. Damn, what possessed you to drive out here in all this mess?"

She looked up at me with a light in her eyes that I had never seen before. "Because I wanted to be with you, Larry," she said softly, and then kissed me.

I think the young people call it a soul kiss. We used to call it French. Whatever it's called now, it sure shook ol' Larry's world up.

Her mouth was wine-sweet and I thought nothing in the world had ever tasted that good. No other lips could be that incredibly soft.

"You crazy kid," I whispered against her mouth. "You're half drunk."

She grinned up at me and returned the whisper. "You crazy middle-aged man." She ran her tongue lightly over my lips. And that produced a sensation I'll never forget. Her tongue was purple from the wine. "You're probably right about that, but who gives a big rat's ass?"

The snow and the sleet and the wind whipped all around and pounded us as we stood in the yard, a white carpet surrounding us. But neither of us made any attempt to seek shelter. She tossed the bottle to the snow, staining it blue/purple.

"Lose your taste for that stuff?" I asked.

"Naw. I just need both hands for this," she replied.

She put her gloved hands behind my head and pulled my mouth down to hers.

After the most blistering kiss I'd ever experienced, I more or less returned to reality. When I found my voice, I said, "Cody, if I had any sense at all, and you did, too, you'd get back in that car and get the hell back to town. Because if you don't, in about five minutes, I won't let you go. The roads will be just too dangerous."

She smiled that sweet, haunting smile. "Well, Larry, if that's the case, old man, I guess I'll just be staying out here with you tonight."

I pushed her back and held her at arm's length. She never looked lovelier than with the snow highlighting that raven hair and the wind reddening her cheeks. It was a picture I'll carry with me all my life.

"Cody, you don't know what you're saying." She opened her mouth to protest and I silenced her. "Listen to me, honey, please. You're half tight. Cody, everything I've said to you has been a lie. Everything. All along. It's all been a plan to get you into my bed. I've lied to you right from the beginning."

The words poured out of me; never had the truth been so bitter and so sweet. I felt as though the years of deceit were washing away with each word.

"I'm no good, Cody. So just please get back into your car and head for town. Do yourself a favor and forget we ever met. Please. I'm a forty-year-old scoundrel. A forty-year-old no-good, lying son of a bitch."

"No, that's wrong, Larry. You're a forty-*one*-year-old scoundrel," she corrected. "Look, you big dummy!" she said, her voice hardened. "I know you've been lying to me. I've known from the beginning. Right from the start. What do you think I am, some sort of fool?"

I stood still as stone for a moment. "What?" I shouted, my yell as loud as the wind that whipped and sang around us, and the wind was wild that winter evening. "You . . . *knew?* You mean . . . you actually allowed me to continue this . . . ridiculous charade? I was making a fool out of myself and you *knew?*"

She laughed at me, her laugh merry and happy and gentle, and, oh, hell, I don't know . . . everything I wasn't, never had been, and didn't deserve. "Sure, Larry. I knew all along. I just wanted to see how far you'd take it." She smiled at me as she lifted her lips to touch mine.

Looking at Cody in the white-rimmed dimness of dusk, I thought how beautiful she was. "But, Cody, I . . ."

"Oh, Larry," she shushed. "Be quiet, old man. You're babbling." She pushed me toward the house. "Ick. You're all wet. Damn, let's get you inside as quick as possible. Man of your advanced age has to be careful. You might catch cold, or something. And I want you to keep your strength up." Behind me, pushing, she giggled.

"Very funny, Cody."

"Yeah. I thought it was."

In the house, she pushed me toward the bedroom. "Go take a hot shower, Larry. You're soaked clear through. If I had known you wanted to play in the snow, I'd have brought my snow-bunny suit. Go on. I've got to get my stuff out of the car."

"Your stuff? What stuff? But . . . I . . ."

"You're babbling again, Larry. Go take a shower. Get into some dry clothes. And please dress the way you normally would. I almost gagged at your rustic act."

"Rustic act," I muttered, marching off to do as I was told, all the while feeling like the world's biggest fool. She had known all along. Jesus! The city slicker got cut off at the knees by the country girl.

By the time I stepped out of the shower, she had laid out all her things on the bed. Jeans and shirt for tomorrow, little boots on the floor. But also on the bed, a light blue, almost diaphanous negligee. There was a noticeable increase in my heart rate and suddenly I was as skittish as an old maid in a men's locker room.

Dressed in what I normally wear for leisure—rustic, I ain't—I walked into the den. "Cody," I said, pointing to the bedroom. "What? . . ."

She patted the floor beside her, in front of the fireplace, and I sat down, our backs to a chair.

"Larry, now it's your turn to listen to me. I wanted everything to be right—you'll see what I mean later on. For I don't know how much time we have."

"Well, no one knows that, Cody. But I don't understand what you mean. If I'm reading all this correctly, and I may not be, we can have a long time together. Forever, even," I added softly. "If that's what you want."

She shook her head. "No, Larry. You're both right and wrong. We don't have a lifetime. And forget forever. Our ages work against us. Your society, your job . . . well, they wouldn't permit it even if we were granted the time. Besides, and please don't take this the wrong way, I'm not sure I want us to have a lifetime . . . together."

I didn't know what in the hell she was talking about. "But, then . . ."

"Hush, Larry." She snuggled up against me. "Let me finish. Yes, I know how you feel . . . finally. I knew, sensed, when your feelings, your motives, changed. Don't ask me how; I just knew. I knew it for a fact last night. When I got home—on the way home—I heard how it was going to snow and maybe the roads would be closing by this evening. So I did my own scheming and planning. You're not the only one who can do that. My aunt is staying with friends. She thinks, they think, I've gone into the city for the weekend." She paused and stared into the flames.

I opened my mouth to speak and then closed it. Don't do it, Larry, I cautioned myself. Just let it drop. Don't say that you finally understood what your heart was saying. You know it's wrong, even though it's right. There was an aching in my heart and a lump in my throat as I looked at her. I tossed all caution aside and for the first time in my life I said the words and really meant them. "Cody?"

"Yes, Larry?"

"I love you, Cody." I had never meant those words as deeply as when I spoke them that night. And I'm equally certain that I never will again.

She sighed. "Yeah. I know you do, Larry."

"Don't bowl me over with your enthusiasm."

She cut her eyes to me and laughed softly. But the laughter held a note of sadness. "It's just . . . well, I'm really afraid, Larry. So very afraid of my own feelings for you."

"You like me, don't you?"

"Oh, Larry—don't be silly. I love you." She spoke those words gently and if a heart could soar, mine did. "I do love you. So, there. I'm glad I could finally say it. But . . . it's confusing. I love you in all kinds of ways. Like a friend, a father, a big brother, and like the love a man and woman should feel. All those feelings all rolled up into one huge emotion. I wanted you so bad the other night it was like a physical pain inside of me. I knew how I felt then, and it scared me. I'm still afraid. This is going to be so right . . . for a time. And then it's going to be so wrong. It's going to end up in a great big mess. I just know it is. Listen to this, Larry. Visualize it if you can: I have this mental picture of us, of me, taking you over to a friend's house, where all my friends gather, and me saying: 'Look, everybody! This is Larry—he's my lover!' That just blows my mind. Can you picture it, Larry? I mean, can you really see it?"

I had to chuckle at the mental picture. Somehow I could not get that scene to focus. It kept fading away, like I was trying to focus through a bad lens. I should have paid attention to that portent—and others—but I didn't.

She studied the expression on my face and read it accurately. "Yeah. Okay. See what I mean, Larry? Old straight-arrow Larry Baldwin, with his conservative haircut, handmade shoes, and expensive custom suits. I'm telling you, Larry, we'd be the hit of the evening. 'Saturday Night Live,' here we come."

Since I have never watched that particular program, I did not have the vaguest idea what she was talking about.

She pressed against me and I put my arm around her. She sighed. "But I do love you," she whispered, with more than a tinge of regret.

We sat for a time in silence, sharing thoughts as we watched the flames dance. I hid a smile as I decided to break the mood. "Well, since we've both bared our souls, so to speak, there's something I have to warn you about, Cody." I spoke as solemnly as possible. "I'll admit, willingly and openly and happily, to being deeply in love with you. I don't know how or why it happened, but it did. However, there is one thing I simply refuse to do, love notwithstanding."

She turned in my arms and stared at me, her eyes serious. "Oh? And what is that?"

"The Funky Chicken!"

"Oh, Larry! You're years behind time." Any tension left between us disappeared with that. She laughed and jumped up, skipping into the open space of the den. I tried to conjure up a picture of me skipping along with her. Didn't work out at all. Another bad image all out of focus.

Then she did one of the most vulgar dances I'd ever seen— and in certain parts of Central America, you can see just about anything, if you have the price of admission.

"This is not quite the Funky Chicken," Cody said. "But will it do?"

I had the disturbing feeling that age wasn't the only thing keeping Cody and me apart. "Good Christ, Cody. Is that a dance you do in public?"

"Come on, Larry," she said, sitting back down beside me. "You're not that old. You were a teenager in the seventies. There was some pretty funky dancing going on back then."

"Not for this kid, Cody."

"You're not joking, are you?"

"No."

"Were you all business back then, too, Larry?"

I smiled at her. "Not necessarily, Cody. I wasn't a monk."

"But you were straitlaced, weren't you?"

"I wasn't very . . . flexible. I never have been. Even as a teenager, I knew what I wanted and set out to get it. I just didn't have time for distractions."

"Is this distracting, Larry?" She leaped to her feet, hands behind her head, her hips undulating. She did a dance that would have put a stripper to shame . . . and had I tried it with her I probably would have thrown my back out and been in bed for a week. "What's the matter, Larry?" Cody asked with a smile. "Are you afraid if you tried it you might like it?"

There was certainly more than a modicum of truth in that. I stared up at her, saying nothing.

She plopped down beside me. "You have any candles, Larry?"

The girl could shift moods faster than the wind. "Candles? Ah . . . yes. As a matter of fact, I do. They were left here in the house."

She pulled me down to the carpet, my arm around her, and kissed me gently. "It's pretend time, Larry. For both of us. I'm a lot younger than you, and a lot less worldly, but I'm not stupid. What I am is a fool for wanting this to happen. And you're a bigger fool for letting it happen. But we both know—knew, I suppose—it was going to happen. So for a time, let's pretend. We'll pretend we're in Paris . . ."

"I'll take you there, Cody."

"Hush. No, you won't, Larry. That won't happen. Except in our minds. Right here in this house. We can be in London, or Switzerland, anyplace but Georgia. This house can be our chalet in the Alps, our chateau outside Paris. For this is all we're ever going to have."

I didn't know what she was talking about. "Cody, it doesn't have to be that way. We . . ."

She silenced me with a kiss, and the touch of her lips was so tender my hardened old heart shattered like fine crystal.

We lay on the carpet for a time, in front of the fire, saying nothing, letting our lips speak volumes. Finally she pulled away and grabbed a throw pillow from the couch, lying back. I propped up on one elbow, content to gaze at her in the flickering light.

She turned her head and put those fantastic pale eyes on me. But there was a twinkle in them, and I knew she was about to pull something. When she spoke, she came on like a young, modern-day Scarlett, laying the molasses on thick.

"Ah won't y'all to know, suh, that you gonna have to court me sum. Y'all gonna have to feed me, pet me, make me feel lak I'm somethang special, and then, and only then, on this heah night, I just might decide to bestow some spacial favors upon you, suh."

"You're nuts, Cody!"

"Suh, ah'll have you know you bes' do what ah tell you to do, now, you heah? Us southern gals kin git right bitchy if'n we set our minds to it."

I gathered her in my arms and she came willingly. "You just tell me what you want, Cody, and I'll do my best to move heaven and earth for you."

Her eyes changed, turning serious for a moment. "Oh, Larry, I'm afraid what I want can never be. Not for very long. But we'll have some memories to keep locked away in special places, to open up and take out and smile about when we're all alone in the years to come."

She was certainly right about that. Both of us would have lots of bittersweet memories for the rest of our lives. I met her serious gaze for a moment. "Are you sure you're not a lot older than you're telling me, Cody? You speak like a much older person—when you want to, that is."

She touched my cheek with her fingertips. "I am what I am, Larry. Just like Popeye. But I warn you now: I am subject to change very quickly." She sighed. "Larry, I don't want either of us to get hurt."

"How do we prevent that?"

"I think . . ." She frowned. "I think we live day by day. Or day to day. We just take things as they come. Let's don't plan on too many tomorrows."

I could see that she was very serious, and doing her best to warn me that she was still young. "All right, Cody. That's the way it'll be."

She laughed suddenly and sat up. "Now, suh, you bes' git crackin' on fixin' me some supper. 'Cause ah'm a right hungry little gal."

"I can handle that."

Her eyes twinkled. "Ever found anything you couldn't handle, Larry?"

"That, Cody, is a loaded question."

"First time for everything."

I wondered what she was trying to tell me.

While Cody spread a tablecloth and set out the silver, I fixed supper.

I had learned to cook early in life. Mother was usually out running around and my dad was drunk by seven o'clock, so with the help of Betty Crocker I taught myself the basics and improved on it over the years. My ex-wife had never fixed a meal in her life—just like her mother. I turned into a good cook and found that I really liked it. On this snowy night, this night that was the beginning of the end for both of us, I fixed Russian food. Contrary to what a lot of Americans have been led to believe, Russian dishes are very good, and Basturma is delicious. It's very simple to prepare, being, in English, nothing more than marinated skewered beef, but it's the basil and the wine vinegar and the lemon that makes it stand out.

Going Russian all the way, I fixed Chrov Plav, which is

rice with fruit and nuts, and for a first course, a soup called Okroshka. I was afraid Cody might not like it, but the way she dug in, she could not have been faking it.

"You really like it, huh?" I asked her.

She waved her spoon. "Don't talk, Larry. Eat."

We cleared the table, rinsed off the dishes, and stuck them in the dishwasher. Cody had lit candles and turned out the other lights, leaving the den in dancing shadows from the fireplace and the candles. We sat on the couch and she snuggled up close to me. I do not recall a time, past or present, when I was happier. We did not speak for a long time, both of us content with the physical closeness. We listened to the wind whipping and moaning around the house.

After a time, Cody sighed and broke the silence. "Want to play the game now, Larry?"

"What game?"

"Where are we?"

The wind sighed around the house and the snow piled up, insulating us from the outside world. Speaking strictly for myself, if we had both died then and there, I would have gone out happy.

I smiled. Okay. I would play her game. "Well . . . how about Russia?"

"All right. We're all alone, in a small cottage, and everything is perfect with us. Right, Larry?"

It certainly was. "Absolutely."

She took my hand and placed it on her breast. I could feel her heart thudding under my palm.

I was content to remain that way. If there were any doubts

lingering in my mind concerning the love I felt for her, they blew away as swiftly as the winds could take them.

"We'll have the time allowed us, Larry," she spoke against my cheek, her breath hot-spiced, her fragrance a perfume that couldn't possibly be duplicated. "And we won't ask for any more than that."

"We can shoot for a lifetime, Cody," I argued gently, the hidden romantic in me leaping to the surface, defending against odds that I did not then know were stacked impossibly high against us.

She put her mouth on mine. "No, Larry. No. We won't have a lifetime. But we can try to make the best of the time that is ours. Please?"

I wondered then, and still do, if she possessed some sort of psychic ability. But I would not argue further with her. We had time. Lots of time. Time for me to convince her that we could have a lifetime, if we so desired.

Cody rose from the couch and prowled the room, blowing out all the candles, plunging us into semi-gloom, the only light left that from the fireplace. Once she looked over at me and smiled shyly. I got the feeling that something was all out of whack here, but I didn't know what.

Then it was time.

I fixed the fire and placed the screen. And waited.

After only a few moments, she called my name, so softly I thought at first I was imagining the sound, thinking the wind was playing tricks on me. I walked into the bedroom and stood in the doorway for a moment. The room was lighted with two long-burning candles. Cody lay on the bed, the covers pulled up to her chin. Her hair fanned out over the white-ness of pillow.

She turned her head while I undressed, then I slipped naked under the covers to lie beside her for a time, only our hands touching. The candles were the scented kind, and the room was filled with the scent of flowers.

She squeezed my hand and whispered, "I want to tell you something, Larry."

I waited.

"Vic Goodman is a liar."

I didn't know exactly what she meant, but I certainly agreed with her about Vic. "Do we have to talk about that ugly toad right at this moment, Cody?"

She paused for a few seconds and then laughed softly. "No. You're right about that. But I just wanted you to know, Larry. I don't want you to be too surprised about me."

"Know what, Cody? What is it about you that's going to surprise me so?" It really seemed like a very inopportune time to be discussing Victor Goodman. His image could put a damper on anything.

We lay side by side for a few moments, and then her reply was a kiss. She hesitated, sighed, and turned and pressed against me. Her breasts burned against my chest. She was all softness in sheer fabric, the heat of her warming the palms of my hands as I touched and caressed her skin. Then with no more than a shrug, the negligee was gone.

The temperature rose in the bedroom, and the candles had nothing to with it. Cody became all fire and movement under my stroking hands and she did not have to say a word to let me know when she was ready.

She slipped under me as she pulled my mouth to hers and whispered, "Please be easy with me at first, Larry. Very, very easy."

"I will be, Cody." After a few seconds, I raised up on my elbows and stared down at her. "Cody?"

"I'm a virgin, Larry."

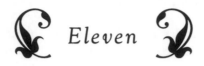 Eleven

Awakening long before Cody, I gently slipped from her soft warmth to pad into the den, quietly adding split logs to the coals and coaxing flaming life to the wood, then turning up the butane heater just a bit. The thermometer on the back porch was holding at a steady thirty degrees and the wind was probably hitting twenty to twenty-five miles per hour with gusts up to thirty-five or so. The snow was coming down hard, creating near-blizzard conditions.

"Good," I muttered. "I don't give a damn if we can't get out for a week."

I slipped back under the covers beside Cody. Her slender arms found me and she snuggled close. I loved the velvet feel of her. She kissed me on the cheek.

"I do love you, Larry," she whispered. "We're a pair of the world's biggest fools for allowing this to happen. But I do love you."

We had loved frantically at first, then slept, her happy tears drying on my shoulder. Awakening, we had loved again, slowly, with all the love in us. And as the wind howled and buffeted the small house, we had then slept deeply, content with each other.

"And I love you, Cody." I kissed her mouth. Both of us positively reeked of love, the musk-scent clinging to the sheets and to us, permeating the room with its bouquet.

"Are the sheep all right?" she asked.

It took me a couple of seconds to grasp the question. Then I realized we were back in Russia. "Yes," I said with a smile. "The sheep are fine."

She stirred and stretched and sighed, naked and warm under the heavy covers. She snuggled closer to me and murmured, "What time is it?"

I glanced at the small clock-radio on the nightstand. "Nine o'clock, honey, and I would have to say that all is most certainly fantastically well."

"Umm," she replied, pushing herself a micro-inch closer. "I sure won't argue that. Say!" Her eyes widened as the wind bounced off and tore around the house. "What's happening out there? Are we having a blizzard?"

"About as close as we can come to one in Georgia." I grinned like a schoolboy. "We might have to stay out here in the country all cooped up longer than we thought. It could be two or three days before the roads are cleared."

"Gee, wouldn't that be terrible?" She twisted in my arms until her mouth was just touching mine and smiled. "I told the people looking after my aunt that I might be gone two or three days. Can you fix it with my boss at the plant?"

"No problem, Cody. It's all taken care of if this weather

keeps on dropping feathers of the angels all over this part of Georgia. The roads will be closed."

"Feathers of the what?"

"Snow. Feathers of the angels."

"That's really very pretty, Larry. You have a poetic side to you."

First time anyone ever said that to me. Larry Baldwin, poet. I grunted in disbelief.

Cody slipped out of my arms and, sitting on the side of the bed, put on one of my shirts and then went padding off to the john. I lay back against the pillows and closed my eyes and thought happy thoughts. The sound of the shower running lulled me off into daydreams and then into full sleep. In those dreams, Cody and I were together, living and loving, happily ever after. Then the dream took a dramatic turn, changing into something more like a nightmare.

The images I had dreamed before were just a bit clearer, more sharply in focus. But they were still foggy in my mind. Vic was there, laughing and holding something. Blue and red flashing lights flickered, making the scene somewhat surreal. People were running and yelling. I could clearly hear the sounds of women crying, weeping uncontrollably. I could see me in the dream, but I could not move. It was as if my shoes were made of heavy blocks of lead, anchoring me to the ground.

I mentally struggled and finally willed myself out of sleep. What the hell had I dreamed? It was the same damn dream as before. I flirted with the thought that it might be an omen, then dismissed that notion. I did not believe in such things—

back then. Before Cody. I pushed all such nonsense away as she emerged from the bathroom.

She stood naked in the room, proud and unashamed of her beauty. She was as close to perfection as I had ever seen. I studied her closely, seeking some blemish, something, anything, to mar the loveliness. There was none that I could find. Her slim legs were perfectly shaped, her waist tiny, her breasts firm.

I watched her dress. A lot of women don't like men to do that, but Cody didn't seem to mind. "Cody," I said. "You're so beautiful."

"Joe Cocker," she replied with a smile.

"I beg your pardon?"

"It's a song. Joe Cocker has this really fantastic version of it. 'You Are So Beautiful to Me.' It's sort of old."

"Yeah. I think I've actually heard that one. Well, you're still beautiful."

"You're probably filled with prejudice," she said, flashing that smile that I'll never forget. "But the lady does thank y'all much. And now, suh, if'n you wouldn't mind too terribly much, would the gentleman kindly haul his ass outta that there bed and take a shower while the lady goes to the kitchen and fixes breakfast?"

I stretched and sighed. "Well, now, Miss Scarlett, the gentleman just might decide to take his morning repast in bed."

She smiled very sweetly at me, and I braced for whatever she had in mind . . . I knew it was something to get me out of bed. For her size, she was very strong and could move very quickly. She jerked the covers off, leaving me stark naked. Then she lifted up one side of the mattress and dumped me on my bare butt on the cold floor. She ran laughing out of the bedroom.

I took a long shower and shaved carefully. When I stepped out of the bathroom, I could smell bacon frying and realized I was ravenous. I dressed and stepped out into the den, standing for a moment, watching Cody move around in the small kitchen.

Make it last forever, I prayed silently to the gods.

"Come get it while it's hot!" Cody called, her back to me.

The lady dished up a very hearty and respectable breakfast and I told her so.

"My mother taught me how to cook," she explained, after covering a piece of buttered toast with jelly. "And it's a good thing she did. If you ever ate anything Aunt Blanche cooked you would probably never want to eat again. It's really grim. Aunt Blanche never could cook worth a crap."

"I was under the impression that people your age lived on junk food."

"Some do, some don't. You and your generation have a lot to learn about young people, Larry." She grinned and that made her look about fifteen years old. It was disconcerting. "You learned something last night, didn't you?" She giggled. "That look on your face was priceless."

I knew what she was talking about. "Hell, Cody. You should have warned me. That was a real shocker."

"Have you ever . . . had a virgin before, Larry?"

"In my youth. Two, I think. Why didn't you tell me, Cody?"

"Oh . . . you wouldn't have believed me. Well, you might have, but no one else would have. You know that. Not after

Vic Goodman's smear campaign. According to him I'm the town whore. Larry, in some respects, adults are more gullible than young people."

I had to agree with that. In some respects. "You're an adult, Cody," I reminded her.

"Yes. I am. But there is no magic line for kids to step over and become adults. One day you're a kid, the next day you're an adult, with all the responsibilities and so forth. No way. It's not fair for society to demand that. Why isn't there a middle ground? Sort of a breaking-in time, an adjustment period?"

I had no answer for that, even though I thought it was a pretty fair idea. "I think a person becomes an adult when they get a driver's license."

"That's kind of hard-nosed, Larry. But I know where you're coming from." She was thoughtful for a moment. "What kind of kid were you?"

I was silent for a moment, thinking back to a youth I seldom bothered to remember. What kind of kid had I been? Born close to the wrong side of town, I came up hardscrabble. Pretty much of a loner. Not really belonging to any one group. I worked at whatever job I could find to make a buck, and had a lot of drive to be more than I was.

"Larry?" Cody prodded softly.

"I heard you."

"You don't like to think about it, do you?"

"Not really. But in answer to your question, I guess I was a tough kid. I had to be."

"I guess you did," she said gently.

A sudden and violent gust of wind hammered the house, rattling the windows.

Cody looked up, toward the draped front windows. "That sounds like it's getting worse, Larry."

"It is. I peeked outside about an hour ago. Let's see what the TV is reporting."

A rare and very major winter storm was upon us, and both the radio and TV were running a list of factories and businesses that would be closed for the duration. The Goodman and Huttle companies were among them. All the schools were shut down. A number of major streets and highways were closed down due to icing. People were being warned to stay home; it was dangerous out there. The cops were stretched thin due to the many automobile accidents.

Cody smiled at me.

The storm was supposed to blow out of the area by late that night, but many of the roads would remain impassable for another day. The temperature would warm up late Monday, and, hopefully, conditions would be back to normal on Tuesday.

Mother Nature had given the two of us an extra thirty-six hours.

"I wonder how we'll pass the time?" I asked innocently.

"Oh, I think you'll probably rise to the occasion," Cody replied.

I decided to let that line die a natural death.

While Cody called the people looking after her aunt, I brought in several armloads of firewood from the back porch, then filled up the woodbox from the outside pile, which I had covered with a tarp.

Cody had fixed a soft pallet on the floor in front of the fireplace, but not too close, and with coffee for me and hot chocolate for her, we lay on the pallet and talked while the storm raged on.

"Is this the way marriage is, Larry?"

"No," I said emphatically. "It most certainly is not. Well," I amended, "maybe for a few months. If the couple is lucky, longer than that. Then . . . it starts to settle down."

"It? You mean routine?"

"Yes, for the most part. And for most couples, unfortunately. It turns into a matter of convenience. But I know a few couples who have made the honeymoon last for years— even a lifetime. I was married, Cody; I told you that." I felt her stir by my side. "But in less than two years, my wife and I were just about total strangers."

"But you stayed together after that. For a time. Why?"

"Habit. We fit well together. She was the perfect executive's wife. She was a professional businesswoman. She knew what to say at just the right time, and to whom. Then . . . well, it was like I said: one day we looked at each other and saw strangers looking back. She knew I was running around on her, and I knew she was running around on me. But we were both very discreet, Cody. That's the name of the game."

She shook her head. "That's sad, Larry."

"Yes. I agree with you."

"You didn't want kids, Larry? I think I asked you that before."

"I would have loved to have children, but she didn't want any. It was best that we didn't. I'm not laying all the blame for the breakup on her. It was fifty-fifty."

"How long were you married?"

"About five years. But in the end, she had her career, I had mine. She had her lovers, I had mine. All in all, it was a lousy marriage."

Cody sipped her hot chocolate and carefully set the mug on the floor. "Was she . . . is she pretty?"

"Beautiful. Very classy lady. Tall and slender."

"Blond?"

"Brunette. Dark, sultry type. Sexy."

"Don't get carried away with it, Dads," she warned, and she was only half-joking.

I laughed at her, but abruptly shut my mouth when I turned my head and got a glimpse of the fire in her eyes. "She was sexy, Cody. Just like you."

"Yeah. Right. I'm a regular sexpot. And don't you forget it. That's the type you like, huh?"

"I like the type I'm with right now, Cody."

"Oh, boy," she said, rolling her eyes. "Cliché time, huh? How many women have you told that, Romeo?" She sat up, locking her arms around her knees and staring at me. Her eyes were very serious.

I didn't have to think about that question for long. "Too many, Cody. Far too many meaningless and fly-by-night affairs. Far too many lies."

"And this—what we have—isn't fly-by-night or meaningless?"

"Oh, no, Cody. This is right. Perfect."

"You're telling the truth?"

"With all my heart."

"Then I believe you."

A faintly disturbing thought came to me. "Cody? Are you on the pill?"

She shook her head. "No. I never saw the need."

"Oh, boy."

She laughed and lay back beside me. "Well, suh, if'n y'all gits me in a family way, I reckon y'all will just have to do the honorable thing."

"Cody, honey, I would dearly love to do the honorable thing. I'd be more than happy to do the honorable thing to-morrow morning if you'd let me."

She touched my face with a small, soft hand. "You really would, wouldn't you?"

"Try me, Cody. Say yes and find out."

She shook her head. "Larry . . . it wouldn't work. So let's not talk about it anymore, okay? Let's just enjoy what we have while we have it."

She kissed me and I said, "I'll bring you around to my way of thinking, Cody. You'll see."

"I'm afraid you will and afraid you won't, Larry."

We sat together on the couch in the den, watching the net-work news on Monday morning. Wars and famine and droughts and floods and car bombings carried out by various criminal types. Then they cut back to the local stations and began showing all the bad weather in the south. I made a rather sexist comment about the female co-host on the show.

Cody very gently put her hand on my crotch and softly squeezed. "What would happen, Larry, if I would really, really squeeze hard?"

"I really, really hope you don't," I said, and meant it fer-vently.

She smiled sweetly, but there was fire in those pale blue

eyes. "Then keep your comments about other women to yourself."

That's how I learned she had a jealous streak.

I look back on that snowy interlude with only the most tender thoughts, even though there would be many more days and nights for us. But not nearly enough of them, not for me. Cody brought to the surface the best I had inside me, and I'll always be grateful to her for that. We would quarrel only occasionally, with no lingering bitterness or rancor. Except for the last quarrel, that is . . . the last time.

But that was in the future, and like Cody said: now is all we have, so let's take it, live it, love it while we have it, for we probably won't have it for long.

Had I any real knowledge of the flat truth of those words, I don't believe I would have allowed the affair to blossom into full, glorious bloom. And if there is any justice in life, any fairness, let it all go to Cody, for she, more than anyone else I know, deserves a decent break.

I had an inkling, of course, of what might lie ahead of us. Those terrible recurring dreams. But I chose to ignore their warnings. I mean, they were only dreams. Who pays any real attention to dreams once one is awake and functioning in the light of day? Not me. Not back then, anyway.

The snow abated that Monday morning, gently tapering off. Cody summed it all up as we stood on the porch of the snowbound house, both of us bundled up against the cold winds.

"It's like we're the only two people left alive in the whole world, Larry. It's like . . . this weekend was made just for us. I know that people have suffered during this storm, and I'm sorry for them but happy for us. Does that make any sense at all to you, Larry?"

"Yes. Of course it does. But there will be other weekends, Cody."

She smiled. "Not like this one, Larry. This one was special. So very special."

I knew what she meant. "I love you, Cody," I whispered against the clean fragrance of her hair. "I really love you."

She turned in my arms and lifted her face upward. "Kiss, please."

I obliged her, and her lips were heartbreakingly soft and sweet. We stood there on the porch, in the cold, locked in a close embrace for a long time, neither of us speaking.

She finally pulled away and looked up at me. "I'm a fool for saying this, Larry, but I love you, too. I wish I didn't. But I do. And believe this, too: I fought my feelings about you. I fought them as hard as I could. I told myself a thousand times this was no good, that it would eventually end up hurting us both. And it will, Larry. It will. But I just couldn't help myself."

"What changed your mind, Cody?"

"You, naturally. You're such a tough, so-called big shot. At least that's what you want people to think. But I found something very different in you, while you thought you were fooling me." She smiled up at me and then laughed, her breath steaming the Georgia cold.

I returned the smile and nodded. "You let it slip at my house that night, didn't you? That night after the local cops leaned on you?"

"About your being lonely? Yes. You have a good memory, Larry. And the other times we talked finally added it all up for me. Others might look at you and see only a tough, ruthless businessman, but I saw lonely in you. I saw a man afraid of his own feelings, who had kept them all bottled up inside for years. You're a person capable of giving, but afraid of giving of himself, 'cause you don't want to be hurt. Love can hurt, Larry. It really can. And I don't want to be the one who hurts you."

"You won't," I assured her. I believed it at the time, and I still believe Cody did not deliberately set out to hurt me. These things just happen.

Her smile was sad in the waning light. "I'm a young person, Larry, and young people can hurt older people without meaning to. But I hope I won't ever hurt you, or that you won't ever hurt me."

"I will never, ever, deliberately hurt you, Cody." I kissed the tip of her nose, which was red from the cold. "I might knock your music, though."

"Yeah?" She pulled back. "Well, that's all you old folks are good for, anyway. Criticize, complain about us kids, and bitch." She pushed up against me. "Well . . . there might be one other thing."

"And that is?"

She told me, using extremely blunt words. I pretended to be in great shock, then told her that was a very good idea.

She agreed.

 Twelve

The weather started clearing early Monday evening, with the temperature rebounding upward. Many of the roads were free of ice and snow by early Tuesday.

I walked around in a besotted fog all day Tuesday. I must have behaved like an idiot. I did not snap, snarl, or growl at anyone at the office. I was nice to everyone. I opened doors for ladies, said Thank you and Please a lot, and in general I was a most charming fellow.

Completely out of character—completely unlike the Larry Baldwin that everyone had come to know and loathe in a relatively short time.

My sudden change caught everyone off guard and confounded all the people at the plant.

It amused Vic. He called me into his office about mid-afternoon and waved me to a chair. He looked at me and giggled. After a weekend with the loveliness of Cody, Vic Goodman was positively grotesque. "Boy," he said, "you in love?"

"Yes," I replied honestly. "Yes, Vic, I really believe I am."

"Lord love a duck! I'd have never believed it of Larry Baldwin if I hadn't been seein' it with my own eyes all damn day. In love! Mercy, mercy me. Is it that little ol' gal from Atlanta, Larry?"

"Yes," I lied, realizing I'd damn well better be very quick on my feet before he asked to meet her. "Or, she was from Atlanta, at least. I put her on a plane to New York this morning. Early. She got a promotion and a transfer."

He frowned. Made him uglier than ever. "Well, hell, Larry-boy—that don't make no sense a-tall. If she done got a transfer, how come you so happy?" He thought about that for a moment, then he grinned. I knew then where the expression "Happy as a hog" must have come from. "Oh, yeah, now I see: all that ice and snow done locked y'all up for three or four days and she done whupped a bunch of that moss on you, right?" He held up a hand. "No offense intended, boy, none a-tall. No, sir."

"None taken, Vic. But you're right."

"Hot damn!" He slapped the desk and the pens and pencils rattled. "I shore like to see my people happy, and you shore are a happy man. Walkin' around grinnin' like a big ol' slop-fed hog. Whoo-boy!" he hollered.

He rambled on for five minutes, exhorting his experiences with love—as he saw and found it. It was nothing like the sensation I was feeling, but I had been where Vic was now. And I knew I would never again sink that low. I managed to smile in all the right places and we were big buddies when I left his office. Comrades in arms. Locker-room assholes.

I resisted an impulse to tell him to screw himself.

———

"I love you, Larry," Cody whispered over the phone. "God, how I love you. I just wanted to call and tell you that."

Tuesday night. "And I love you, Cody. When can I see you again?" I felt like a sophomore in high school and was probably behaving like one.

"This weekend. We'll spend the entire weekend together. But let's not call or see one another 'til then. Let's give this time to cool off just a little—okay?"

"For one reason only, Cody."

"Oh?"

"I want to see if this delicious feeling of . . . well, this euphoria will fade or endure and flourish."

"Oh, yes, Larry. That's the way I feel, too. I've been walking into walls all day long. The other girls in the office were all laughing at me. Larry, I've never felt anything like this in my whole entire life. This is really, really love. It's . . . well, wonderful. But not like when I was in junior high. You know what I mean?"

"Yes, I do, Cody."

"I love you, Larry-Big-Shot."

"And I love you, Cody-Kid."

She was laughing as she hung up.

I thought the weekend would never arrive. The days seemed to contain twice the number of hours, and the nights were even worse. But strangely, the ache, the longing, was not all physical. And because of that, I knew I truly loved the young woman. And quite frankly, that scared the hell out of me, bringing me awake in the dark, quiet hours, thinking hard thoughts, searching the inner depths of my mind and soul.

Was I feeling guilt for having fallen in love with someone so much younger than I? I didn't think so then and even now, after the lonely years, I don't feel that way. I honestly felt it was right and open and decent.

Finally, in a dream, I tore down the last barrier in my mind and heart and admitted: Yeah, I'm in love. Right or wrong, good or bad, I'm in love. So give me the dice and stand back, 'cause the point I'm trying to make in this crap shoot is a hard one. And God! that table looks so long and green. I can't even see the other end.

And the spectators that crowded the table were not the usual noisy, boisterous, laughing, cheering-me-on types. These people were silent, grim-faced, with open hostility and disapproval on their faces. They stood quietly by the long table, placing their bets . . . all betting against me. The damn dice were so heavy I could hardly lift them, but I managed to get them in my hand, determined to toss them. I shook the dice and the clicking sounded like a death rattle. I drew my hand back to toss them and once more looked toward the end of the long table. Cody stood there in bloody clothing, her face bruised and torn and swollen. She held out her hands and they were bleeding.

I dropped the dice in horror and the nightmare faded . . .

Then that other dream came rolling in, all foggy and misshapen and shrouded in mystery. But somehow I knew it was early morning in the recurring dream. Pre-dawn. The lonely time. Those same strange damn flashing lights seemed to be a bit brighter this time around. There was Vic, laughing and holding something and pointing. In my dream, I strained my eyes to see what he was pointing at, but could not make it out.

But I could hear the sounds of crying more clearly now, and could easily make out the crowd that had gathered. They stood silently, staring at . . . I couldn't make it out.

I fought through the dreams and upon awakening, managed to put them completely out of my mind. Almost. Bad dreams, or not. Omen, or not. It was Friday.

I must have walked fifty miles in the den of the house between three o'clock and seven that evening. I cursed myself for behaving like a damned childish fool. The cursing did not help or hurry the waiting. Not a bit. Only one thing would heal the bruise on my heart: Cody.

I was almost in a state of panic when the headlights of her little car finally cut the darkness of the pines. I met her halfway up the walk and felt the splash of her tears as I kissed her under the cold, impersonal glitter of the stars.

We both started talking at once and she put a gloved hand to my lips and shushed me. "Larry, ever since we talked Tuesday, I've been telling myself what a fool I am, what a bad thing this is, for both of us. I told myself as I packed this afternoon, and I told myself on the way out here. But I just couldn't make myself go back." She flung her arms around my neck and kissed me. "I love you, Larry. I honestly, genuinely love you."

I kissed the tears from her face. "I've been pacing the floor like a madman waiting for you, Cody. I was almost ready to believe time had stopped."

"It would be better for the both of us if it had," Cody said, her eyes serious. "But I do know the feeling, Larry. Believe me, I do."

I carried her things inside and buttoned up both cars, after tucking them behind the house, on the circle drive. The drapes were thick and expensive; no light penetrated. During the day the house was difficult to see from the road because of the many trees. At night, with the drapes pulled, it was impossible.

She curled up in her chair by the fire while I lit the coals in the grill on the back porch. Then, a martini for me, a glass of wine for her. I sat in my chair and we lifted our glasses.

"To us, Larry," Cody said. "And I really mean that. With all my heart, I mean it."

I lifted my glass. "I'll certainly drink to that."

She drained her glass, then smiled, her usual good humor fast returning. "Do I get to toss the glass into the fireplace?"

"You get to do anything your heart desires, Cody." I would have attempted to catch the wind for her if she had asked for it.

She tossed the glass into the fire, shattering it. "I made a wish, Larry."

"Going to share it with me?"

She nodded her head slowly. "I wished for us . . . happiness. I wished . . ." She sighed, the expression on her face, in her eyes, sad. "I wished this could go on forever." She looked at me, her eyes glistening with sudden tears. "And I guess that makes me a fool, doesn't it, Larry?"

"It makes you human, Cody. It just took me a lot longer to get there." I left my chair to kneel by her, my hand seeking hers.

She squeezed my hand. "It's kind of like that poem. You probably know it: *to love and be loved by me.*"

" 'Annabel Lee.' One of my favorites."

"Can you recite it?"

"I remember parts of it."

"Say it to me, please."

I sat on the floor and put my memory banks to work. My voice broke on the verse about the angels in Heaven, the demons down under the sea, and about never dissevering his soul from the soul of the beautiful Annabel Lee.

Cody slipped from her chair to sit beside me and put her arms around my neck. Her tears dampened my face.

"Hey, now, Cody-kid. This is no way to start a weekend. Maybe we ought to get up and do the Funky Chicken."

She laughed, wiped her eyes, and kissed me.

We did the Funky Chicken, all right, but it was not to the beat of any recording pushing through the speakers in the den. While the charcoal turned into cold white ash in the grill, and the steaks lay forgotten in the refrigerator, the two of us shoved all the day-to-day woes of the world away and sought comfort in each other's arms.

The weather forecasters say the temperature slipped into twenty-two that night. So did I, in a manner of speaking.

While the wind sighed and sang its cold melody across the land, we composed and rehearsed and perfected our own melody of love. And if only for a few hours, the silence broken solely by the sighs and whispers, the song became a classic for both of us.

In the early hours of Saturday morning, we awakened as one being: a large, very hungry animal. I cooked up bacon and eggs and fried potatoes while she fixed a soft pallet on the floor in front of the fireplace.

After gorging ourselves, we dumped the dishes in the sink and headed for the pallet. We made love as if it was to be our last time, finally falling asleep in a tangle of blankets and warm flesh.

"Next week, Cody," I suggested over a very late breakfast, "let's take off for San Francisco."

She looked up. "That would be far too expensive, Larry."

"I can afford it."

She was silent for a moment, then she shook her head. "I like it here."

I studied her face for a heartbeat, then asked, "What's the matter, Cody?"

She put her small, smooth hand on my big right paw, the knuckles still faintly bearing the scars from long-ago fights. "Let's keep what we have, Larry. It's going to spoil soon enough without any pushing from either of us."

My expression was decidedly bleak and she picked up on my mood, squeezing my hand.

"Cody, why are you such a constant harbinger of doom and gloom?"

"Because I don't want to see you hurt, that's why?"

"Would you please explain that?"

"Age, Larry. The difference in our ages. A few years do separate us, you know," she added drily. "People will give you funny looks and make shitty comments behind your back. Our backs."

"We'll be going to a very sophisticated city, Cody. To high-class hotels and restaurants where people mind their own business. There aren't any rednecks in downtown San Francisco and none where we'll be staying."

She nodded her head in agreement. "I'm sure all that is true, Larry. We'll go someday, maybe." There was an evasive note to her offer. "But not now."

I detected a note of finality in her tone that clearly warned me to drop the issue. I wondered if Cody might be embarrassed about the difference in our ages. But I also knew better than to ask. "Would you like to drive into the city today, Cody?"

"No."

"What would you like to do?"

She rose from the table and rinsed her plate. She poured me another cup of coffee and stood by my chair, her hand on my shoulder. "You might think this is silly."

"Try me."

"I would like just to be with you, Larry. Sit close to you while you tell me all about yourself, the places you've been, the things you've done, the things you've seen."

I looked up into a pair of very serious eyes. "I just offered to show you one of those places, Cody."

"I'd rather hear about it from you, Larry."

Her expression said she would brook no more argument. I nodded. "All right. Then that's the way it will be, Cody. I only want to see you happy."

In the den, we sat on the sofa, her hand resting on my thigh. "Would you believe I'm happier now than I've ever been in my whole life, Larry?"

"Yes. But it's a bittersweet happiness, isn't it, Cody? Am I right?"

She sat silent for a time, then nodded her head. "Yes. It's a feeling that I don't understand."

"I know. I have the same feeling."

"Is it good or bad?"

I hesitated in replying and for once she did not pick up on it. "I don't know that, either."

There was no trace of the storm left on Sunday, and it turned out to be an unusually warm and spring-like day. We strolled down to the creek about noon to sit on a bench by the bank. For a time we said nothing, content just to be together.

Cody threw a pebble into the water and broke the silence. "The time seems to go by so fast when we're here. It seems like I just drove out a few hours ago. Does life go by this fast all the time?"

I started to tell her it damn sure did once you hit thirty, but I bit that off short. "Yes. It goes by at a pretty rapid clip, Cody. And it seems to pass much more quickly when people are happy."

"Are you happy, Larry?"

"I've never been happier, and that's the truth."

"You have many regrets in your life, Larry?"

I had to smile and sigh at that question. "Well, I didn't think so, up until a few weeks ago."

She waited for me to continue. When I remained silent, she moved closer and touched my arm. "So what happened then?"

I looked at her. "You happened, Cody. I started evaluating what I had become—perhaps what I've always been. You're a good person, Cody. You brought on all that retrospection and soul-searching. And . . . I guess I haven't been such a good person for many years. If I ever really was."

"Oh, that's crap, Larry. It really is. If I'm such a good person, then what am I doing out here with you, shacked up with a man nearly twice my age?"

I chuckled at her bluntness. "That's not the kind of *good* I mean, Cody, and you know it."

She shrugged her shoulders and made a face.

"Let's play 'what if,' Cody."

She grinned at me. "How do you play that? Is that some sort of sex game? Damn, L.J., you're worse than a goat!" But she couldn't carry it through and burst out laughing.

"No, Cody, it's not a sex game. Tell me, what would you do if you were to run over a dog or cat on the highway, or just came up on a dog or cat that had been hurt?"

"What a horrible question! Why . . . I'd stop, of course. Try to see if I could help the poor thing."

"And if it were alive?"

"I'd take it to a vet."

"At your own expense?"

"Why, sure." She seemed offended at the question, as if that were the normal thing to do, that everybody would do that. Sure, they would. Right. About one out of every five hundred people, or so. If that.

"And if you saw a beggar on the street with his or her hand out, asking for money?"

"If I had any to spare, I'd give that person some money. It might not be much, but I'd give something. Providing they weren't drunk or really aggressive. Sure. I'd help a hungry person get something to eat. Wouldn't you give a homeless person some help, Larry?"

"Hell, no. No way. Not the old Larry Baldwin. The bastards can, by God, go out and find a job, just like everyone else."

Cody looked at me for several heartbeats. "Sometimes, especially these days, jobs can be hard to find. Larry, you're just not that cruel and heartless."

Oh, but I was. Before Cody. I let that remark slide. "And I bet you go around helping to gather up toys for poor kids at Christmastime, don't you?"

"Yes," she said softly. "I sure do."

I knew she did. "Tell me this, Cody: who's your favorite person at the local nursing home?"

"Why, that would be Mrs. Pearson. She . . ." Cody shut her mouth as she realized I'd trapped her.

"Most of the people I know, and probably many that I don't know, wouldn't and don't do any of those things I just mentioned, Cody. Believe it. Now, do you still question the fact that you're a good person?"

Cody stared at the small creek for a moment. "You really wouldn't stop to help a hurt dog or cat, Larry?"

The question was softly spoken, but with very noticeable heat behind the words. My reply had damn well better be the right one, and I knew it.

"An animal, yes, I would. Giving money to everybody who has their hands out, no. Many homeless voluntarily chose that way of life. And I haven't figured out a way to tell the difference."

"I get the picture, Larry. I see what you mean. But you've

just confirmed what I thought all along: you're really a very complicated man."

"Not really, Cody. I just bring it all down to the basics. But what I am is a better man since I met you." I looked into her eyes. I could never get enough of them. "And I thank you for that."

She smiled at me and shivered.

"Are you cold?"

"Not really. I just hate winter. You know why I hate winter, Larry?"

"You can't wear a bikini and prance around the beach, maybe?"

"I don't even own a bikini! No. That's not it. It's because there are no butterflies."

"They migrate, Cody."

"Do they really?"

"Yes. The Monarchs migrate down to a high mountain ridge in Mexico. Every fall. All of them. Millions of them. They return in the spring. I'm told it's a beautiful sight to see. And that's about all I know concerning butterflies." But I love one special butterfly with a velvet touch. And I knew what I was going to get Cody for her birthday. I'd seen one once, and it was a gorgeous piece of work. And now that I knew she loved butterflies, it would be the perfect present.

"Millions and millions of butterflies," she said. "Wow! What a sight that must be."

"I imagine it is."

"I sure would like to see that place someday."

"Maybe you will, Cody. I hope so."

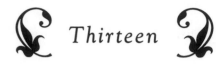 *Thirteen*

I called nearly every jewelry store in Atlanta before someone finally told me they had what I was seeking. I had
them describe it for me, then told them to hold it—I'd be
coming in that Friday to pick it up.

Leaning back in my chair at the office, I smiled. Alto-
gether, it was going to be a swell weekend. I mentally reviewed the past few days. Vic was out of town, gone up to
Canada, profits were up for the company, my stockbroker had
just called and told me I had made a very vulgar sum of
money—due to his expertise, of course—all the salespeople
were producing well, the weekend was coming up—and I was
in love.

My secretary buzzed me. "Mr. Goodman on the phone,
sir."

"Shit," I said.

I heard the secretary laugh just as I was picking up the
phone. She had heard my one-word comment and felt the
same way.

"Yeah, Vic?"

"Howdy there, boy. Land sakes, Larry. It's colder than a witch's tit up here!"

I sighed. It was hog-calling time again.

Just as I was leaving for Atlanta, I spotted Mike Goodman in his latest toy—bought, of course, by his father. It was a customized pickup truck, one of those massive jobs that sits high off the ground on huge tires about four or five feet high. I have never understood why anybody would want one of the damned things, what good they are, or why they are even legal.

But Mike had one, and even if they weren't legal for road use, no one except maybe a state trooper would bother him—not in Vic Goodman's county.

I had never been formally introduced to Mike, and had no desire to meet him, but I had heard a lot about him—and not just from Cody. None of what I had heard was good. But I had seen him on numerous occasions. I didn't like him at first glance. He was in his early twenties and appeared to be in good physical shape. He was a well-built young man, good-looking in a pretty-boy way. He'd be even better looking if he didn't have a constant sneer on his lips.

I had pulled over to get gas and after filling the tank, I sat and watched as Mike roared into the drive-in cafe across the street, squalling the huge tires and acting like someone about fifteen. He walked with a swagger.

"There's a young man who's not just asking for trouble," I muttered. "He's begging for it."

I put the punk out of my mind and drove into Atlanta. I

was looking forward to seeing the expression on Cody's face when I gave her the present.

"Larry, it's so beautiful," she whispered. "But . . . I can't take it. It must have cost a fortune. Please take it back and get something silly for me."

It was expensive. Very. Several thousand dollars worth of expensive, but I wasn't about to tell Cody that. The gift was a gold watch in the dainty, delicate shape of a butterfly, diamond studded.

I lifted her chin with my fingertips. There were tears in her eyes. "Cody, you spent much more than you could afford on my present. I assure you, I can well afford this, and I want you to have it."

Her kiss was tremblingly gentle, and I will always recall that moment with something very close to physical pain.

"All right, Larry," Cody said. "I'll take it and wear it because you want me to. Nobody ever gave me a present I'll treasure so much."

I couldn't think of anything else to say, so I kept my mouth shut.

Dinner was a rather steamy affair, with much meeting of the eyes, much hand-touching, and Lord help me, slipping off our shoes and playing footsie under the table. I hadn't even done that when I was a kid.

We didn't scrape the dishes. Hell, we didn't even clear the table. Just rose as if under the same silent command, blew out the dinner candles, and walked silently into the bedroom.

Our lovemaking that night was slow and measured, with just the quietest of murmurings, the softly spoken words and gentle caresses of lovers in love, and later, the deepest, most peaceful sleep I had experienced in a long time.

Saturday morning, Cody was very quiet, almost subdued. She kept looking at her watch, touching it. I waited, knowing she would tell me what was on her mind when she was ready. She stood in the small kitchen, gazing out the window at the cold rain that had begun during the love-filled night, out in the country, in the house by the wandering creek.

"Like diamonds," she finally spoke.

"What is, Cody?" I asked from the table, where I sat drinking coffee.

"The rain." She spoke with her back to me, still looking out the kitchen window. "When it hangs on the bare branches, just before the drops fall away. They're like lost diamonds, then they smash on the ground. And then they're gone," she added softly.

I said nothing. Cody's mood swings could be very wide, and she was suddenly contemplative. I knew to leave her alone. I watched her and waited.

She turned from the rain-spotted window, catching me looking at her. Our eyes met, locked, held. She finally said, "What happens to us, Larry?"

"Enlarge the question, Cody."

"You know what I mean."

"I think that's entirely up to you. I've made it very clear where I stand."

Her eyes held a strange look. "I'm going to be off from next Thursday noon until the following Tuesday. Plant shutdown."

I waited for her to drop the other shoe. I knew why the

plant was closing, only operating a few days a week. Bernie had told me: they were deep in the red. The economy was not in real good shape, and even some huge companies were suffering the effects. Nationally, the Huttle Company was in good shape, but locally they were hurting. Trade talk was they might not pull out of it. Either way, it was going to be a squeaker.

"Well, then, Cody, we can have a long weekend."

"Can you get off, Larry?"

"Sure. No problem."

She looked at her new watch, and then at me. I thought I saw mist in her eyes. "You want to know where we're going, Larry? Us. Together. Really know?"

"I believe that was your question, Cody."

"Answer me, Larry. Please?"

"All right. Yes. I'd really like to know what's in your head, Cody."

"If you can get the time off, and the offer is still open, let's go to San Francisco. It was your idea, remember? I want to prove something to you, and to myself, I suppose."

I looked down at my coffee cup. "You sound like this is make or break time."

She shook her head. "I don't think it's that bad. But I would like to see how we fit in public. It's for you as much as for me."

"You mean it?"

"Absolutely."

I nodded in agreement. She was right. Let's see how we look and feel and fit out in the light. All we had done so far was hide like moles. "You'll love the city, Cody."

"We'll see," was her only response.

Her mysterious attitude put only a slight damper on just a very small part of the day, then she began to snap out of it. It was picturing us in public, I assumed, although knowing Cody, that was not all that was troubling her. She might or might not get around to telling me the whole story.

Cody insisted on fixing dinner that evening—she'd brought out a sack of groceries—and she also insisted that I stay the hell out of the kitchen.

Of course, I peeked in from time to time. She was a study in concentration as she prepared the meal, biting her lower lip, frowning as she worked. The food smelled delicious and it was. I ate like a pig.

"You really like it, don't you?" Cody asked.

"I sure do. You're a good cook."

"Wait 'til you see what I have for dessert."

"Oh?" She knew I rarely ate dessert.

She grinned lewdly and rolled her eyes.

"I can't imagine what it is."

She looked a bit crestfallen.

"Have I had it before?"

She called me a very ugly name, shot me the bird, and marched off to the bedroom. I ate the rest of my dinner, figuring I would need all the strength I could muster. I had discovered that Cody was highly sexual and very inventive, and she was not the least bit inhibited.

When I walked into the bedroom, she was lying naked on the bed. She pointed to one breast. "Start here, L.J. You know the rest of the route."

We took the early afternoon flight out of Atlanta, heading for the city by the Bay. Cody was dressed in a conservative outfit and looked very much the lady. I suspected she had done it in an attempt to smooth out the age difference, although the two-decade gap was still evident. Just not as much as before.

Before we left the country house, Cody had carefully inspected herself in the mirror, turning this way and that. "How do I look, Larry?"

"At least forty."

"Get serious, Baldwin. Come on—how do I look?"

"Oh, I'd say . . . like maybe you just graduated from a doctoral program at Princeton."

"Then I added a couple of years, right?"

"Yeah. But there was no need to."

"I did it for me, too, Larry."

It was Cody's first flight, but whatever anticipation she felt, she hid it well. We were in first class, and the flight attendant—herself not more than a couple of years older than Cody—picked up on the relationship on her first pass through. They've seen it all, though, and other than a slight smile, she made no other gesture as she spotted Cody's hand resting on my thigh.

When we were airborne at cruising altitude, and the color had returned to Cody's face and she was breathing normally again, she went to the restroom. On the way back to her seat, she spoke for a few minutes with the flight attendant, who glanced in my direction a few times. When Cody was again belted in, I asked if she'd made a new friend.

"She asked about us."

I waited. "And?" I prompted.

"I told her."

Again, I waited. "And?"

"She said it looked like damn nice work if a girl could get it. She was looking."

"Jesus! Cody, you talked for about five minutes. What else was said?"

"Nosy, aren't you?" she said with a smile.

"Give!"

"Oh . . . girl stuff. This and that. You really wouldn't be interested."

"Try me."

She whispered in my ear.

"You've got to be kidding!"

She shook her head. "Nope."

"Jesus! Is nothing sacred?"

Cody smiled.

I never did know if she was kidding or not.

As far as I'm concerned, San Francisco is still a beautiful city. Yeah, I know the lady is getting a bit soiled and a bit gamey in spots, but she's still a grand gal. And I had four full days there with Cody.

I had reserved a suite in advance, and when we checked in, the desk clerk, a man I had known for several years, didn't make a bobble.

"Enjoy your stay with us, Mr. Baldwin."

"Thank you, Charles. I'm sure we will."

On the elevator up, Cody said, "You know that slick-lookin' peckerwood at the desk, baby?"

She was about to pull something for the benefit of the others in the elevator. She had a wicked gleam in her eyes and a slight smile on her lips. I braced myself.

"For years, honey," I said.

"Yeah? I get it. You've brought other women up here before, right?"

A half-dozen eyes slid toward us, then clicked forward again, staring at the door. The ladies with us were, according to their name tags, with a group of people attending some sort of religious convention. This was right up Cody's alley.

"Yeah, I have. Every time I'm in the city, baby. But never one as expensive as you. Five hundred bucks is absurd. How much of that does your pimp get?"

Cody winked at me.

"Good Lord, Ruth!" a rather ample lady whispered hoarsely behind us. "Did you hear that?"

"Yes," Ruth returned the whisper.

"Never mind what my old man gets," Cody said. "But I'll tell you this, for what you're getting, five hundred is cheap. Goin' around the world is hard work. I just hope you can keep it up for me."

"I believe I'll get off here," a lady said.

The others elected to stay.

"Hell, baby," I said. "Five hundred bucks would damn near take me around the world—literally."

"Not with this cruise director, baby," Cody retorted. "Did you bring the leather and the whips?"

Ruth and friend looked at one another, horror in their eyes. Ruth said, "Sodom and Gomorrah, Rebecca. We're witnessing it firsthand. I'll pray for the both of you," she informed us.

"I would appreciate it, lady," Cody told her. "It's a damn rough life. I probably won't be able to walk tomorrow."

"Heavens!" Ruth cried.

Luckily, our floor was next and the door opened before Cody could say any more.

In the suite, the late afternoon sun pouring through the windows; we convulsed with laughter, hanging onto each other. I had not laughed so much in years. My ex-wife would have been completely mortified by the exchange in the elevator. I loved it, realizing then just how repressed I had allowed myself to become over the years.

Cody looked at me and said, "I think, Larry, for the sake of your reputation, we'd better skip the hotel restaurant while we're here."

And that set us off again, howling like crazy, clinging to each other in the middle of the elegant suite, set against the backdrop of San Francisco. One thing led to another, and suddenly the bed seemed to be the most logical place for us. Little piles of clothing marked our trail and we spent the first late afternoon and early evening in the city doing some exploring of our own, and on our own.

At full dark, we stood naked by the huge window, me behind Cody, my arms wrapped around her. We gazed out at the multicolored lights of the city and the moving darkness of the bay.

"It's so beautiful, Larry," Cody whispered. "So lovely. It's everything you said it would be."

"And a lot more, Cody. Tomorrow, we'll rent a little sports car, a convertible maybe, and drive the coastline highway to the winery section. We'll get a picnic lunch and eat by the cliffs and listen to the waves crash."

"And?" she asked, turning in my arms, pressing all her nakedness against me.

"Love each other."

"Super!" she said in a gentle whisper. Her mouth was sweet and her skin like satin. And somehow we both forgot about dinner.

Fourteen

When Cody came out of the dressing room of the exclusive dress shop the next morning, I just stood and stared at her for a moment. It was as if I was seeing a totally different person. And in a way, I was.

"She's absolutely stunning, Mr. Baldwin," the saleslady said. "You're a very lucky man."

She was right on both counts. Cody seemed to be made for expensive clothing. The cocktail dress fit her perfectly, highlighting every curve, accentuating her perfection.

She did a little pirouette and smiled at me, then whispered, "Larry, this dress and those others must have cost a ton of money."

I had to blink at that. "Don't you like them? You picked them out."

"Oh, I love everything. But that isn't what I said—asked."

"They're all you, Cody. You're made for these things."

She blushed, and that was rare. "I thought you liked me *au naturel?*"

"I prefer you . . . well, I just prefer you."

She looked around and then gave me a quick kiss.

"You'd better go pick out something else, Cody. Before I take a notion to attack you right here, right now."

"I bet that would give the ladies something to talk about," she said with a grin. "I can just see me bent over the back of that silly-lookin' little ol' couch yonder with this fancy dress all hiked up and you plowin' the back forty."

My laughter rang out all over the shop and heads turned. "Cody, you're incorrigible!"

She patted her hair and curtsied. "Pretty, too."

She was all of that. In a city of beautiful women, even the maitre d' almost fell all over himself escorting us to our table at one of the most exclusive restaurants. Cody turned every male head in the room while their wives or girlfriends shot her daggers. Even the male couple looked envious.

"Dream on, boys," I muttered. One waggled his fingers at me and the other winked.

Cody caught it and silently mouthed something very vulgar at the pair and they got all upset. She looked at me and simpered, "You are pretty, Larry."

I sighed. "Don't start, Cody. Just cool it."

"Yes, suh, boss."

Cody had gone to a beauty salon that afternoon and when she emerged with a new hairstyle, she had added a couple of years—again, her idea, not mine—and the stylist had somehow enhanced her beauty. She looked almost the same, but there was a subtle difference. I asked what it was.

"You wouldn't understand, Larry. Men never do. Just accept it and be quiet."

"Yes, ma'am."

For a small-town Georgia girl, Cody had impeccable manners. But I wasn't fooled for a second. I knew her too well by now. I knew how she loved to shatter pomposity, to prick the balloon of pretense. She was the very quintessence of loveliness and grace and charm, but if anyone crossed her, she could open that lovely mouth and let them have it with a string of cuss words that would embarrass a drunken dockworker.

She must have picked up on my anxiety, for she patted my hand and said, "Relax, Rhett. This heah li'l ol' southern gal done put on her bes' face for this evenin' out. Ah wouldn't do nothin' to 'barrass y'all in front of all these highfalutin' gentry types." She smiled sweetly.

I returned the smile. "Why is it, Cody, that your remark does so little to assuage my doubts?"

That sweet smile set in that heart-shaped face held more than a touch of mischief. "Ah done tole y'all, suh, I's just me. And ah seems to recall that y'all done tole me that you din' want this heah gal to change none. Ain't that a pure-dee fact, now, suh?"

"That is correct, Miss Scarlett."

"Sho'nuff is." She tasted her wine and made a horrible face. "This stuff tastes like sheep shit smells!" she whispered. Unfortunately, the wine steward was standing only a few feet away.

He spun around, glaring at her. He had chosen the wine personally and the insult he felt at her remark was evident on his face. "Perhaps," he said haughtily, "the mademoiselle would prefer some warm milk?"

Cody looked at him and smiled. I knew both the look and the smile and what could follow. She wiggled a finger at him. The index finger, I noticed with a sigh of relief. He stepped closer and leaned over.

"Fuck you, dude," Cody whispered.

He straightened up quickly, his face red. "I beg your pardon!"

"You'll figure it out," she told him.

"Well!" he huffed, then spun around and marched off, his back ramrod stiff.

"Walks funny, too," Cody remarked, munching on a piece of bread.

I shook my head and chuckled.

"I should have ordered a biscuit and salt pork sandwich and a bowl of grits in this joint," Cody said. "And a glass of buttermilk. Except that crap tastes worse than the wine."

I touched her hand. "Cody . . . don't ever change."

"I'll make a deal with you, Larry."

"Lay it on me, Cody."

" 'Lay it on me?' " She laughed. "Okay. This day is yours. We do whatever you want to do. You want to go to a concert, the opera, a museum, I'm with you and I'll do my best to enjoy it. If I don't, you'll never know. But tomorrow is mine, and you tag along with me. Okay?"

"It's a deal."

"Great. Where do we go and what should I wear?"

I put my hands on her shoulders. "Now, Cody, you really don't believe I would subject you to an opera, do you?"

"You like it, don't you?"

"Yes. I enjoy the opera."

Her shoulders shifted under my hands. "Then I'll try to enjoy the opera, Larry. If that's what you want, it's fine with me."

She really meant it, but I shook my head. "Maybe sometime, Cody. Opera is not something the unfamiliar should just jump into. It's like brandy or a martini or fine wine . . . you acquire a taste for it slowly. So . . . I know you like lovely things. Have you ever been to an art gallery?"

She screwed her face up until she looked like something out of Lady Macbeth's worst nightmare. I grimaced at the sight. "No," she said in mock seriousness. "I reckon not. You see, Pine Hills is really sorta short on those types of things. But when I was a kid, I used to listen to the Grand Old Opry, though. And I have played Putt-Putt golf."

"Cody, will you kindly return your face to some sort of normalcy? I would be forever grateful. Thank you. I'm so glad your cultural background is so extensive."

"Right. So we're going to an art gallery."

"A museum, actually."

"Well, let's hit the trail, Dads."

She loved it. There was a particularly fascinating exhibit in one area and Cody was thrilled with it. To my delight and amazement, she skipped right past the surrealistic and other "way-out" forms of so-called art, and stayed with the traditional and the work of the masters—what I prefer, too.

A painting by Caravaggio held her attention for a long time. She viewed it from every possible angle. It was here on loan and entitled *The Musicians*. "I really like this one, Larry."

"It's said that Caravaggio lacked organization and dealt with sentimentality," I told her, reading from a pamphlet. "Also that the work that began with him and others of his period finally sank into the melodrama and extravagance of the Baroque period."

She looked at me for several seconds, silent exasperation on her face. "Well, no shit, Sherlock! I happen to like it. How old is that thing?"

"About four hundred years."

"Super."

We spent hours wandering in the museum, until Cody glanced at her butterfly watch. "Damn, Larry. Where'd the time go? It's the middle of the afternoon."

"I thought you'd like it here."

"I owe you several hours."

"What? I beg your pardon? What do you mean, you owe me several hours?"

"That's the way it's going to be from now on, Larry. Fifty-fifty all the way down the line."

"I'm . . . still not sure what you mean."

"This afternoon was as much fun for me as it was for you because of the paintings. Tell you the truth, I probably enjoyed it more than you did, and I want to come back someday. So tomorrow, I owe you hours. Now do you see what I mean?"

"I guess so, Cody."

We had walked outside and were standing in the cool afternoon air.

"No, you don't," she said. "Not really. So I'll level with you. Larry, my aunt is going into a home for the elderly. The neighbors and the doctor finally convinced me that would be the best thing for her . . . and for me. I guess I've known it for several months. There are whole days when she doesn't know me. It scares her and it scares me. I just can't take it any longer. I'm afraid she's going to burn the house down. It's almost happened twice. She's reached the point where she's got to have constant care and I can't stay home and take care of her and I can't afford to hire private nurses. When I told Dr. Averett I didn't want to be there when they . . ." Her voice caught. ". . . When they took her away, he said he was going to suggest that I go away for a few days so it wouldn't confuse Aunt Blanche further. So . . . there were two reasons why I wanted to come out here with you. I just told you one of them. I thought you'd have enough sense to figure out the second one."

The look on my face must have been one of utter confusion. At that point I could certainly empathize with Aunt Blanche.

"Larry! Are all men as dense as you? Or as you appear to be at this moment? Good God! For a smart business person you sure are dumb at times."

I took her hand in mine and we walked for half a block in silence. "Cody . . ."

"Oh, shut up, Larry. Let me talk. I make more sense at a time like this. All right, I will admit I went a full one hundred and eighty degrees in my thinking. I really believe we're in for a rocky time of it, but I love you, you big dummy, so I'm willing to give it a try. We won't talk about marriage, but I will live with you, if you still want me to."

All my attention was riveted on Cody and I walked smack into a street lamppost and banged my knee. "Goddammit!" I leaned against the post for a moment, rubbing my aching knee. "Are you serious, Cody?"

People paused to look at us, some walking on, others staying to watch, smiling. We paid them no attention.

"Just as serious as a crutch, baby." Cody looked at me and smiled. "Which is what it looks like you need right about now. How's your knee?"

"It hurts."

She shook her head. "Man gets to be your age and can't see where he's going maybe ought to think about getting glasses. Or a seeing-eye dog."

"Don't be a smartass, Cody." I continued to rub my knee. It was a little better.

"Why not? I have been all my life. I'm not going to change just for you, Dads. Besides, I guess you need someone to look after you. Grown man walks into great big pole." She was struggling to keep from laughing. "Pitiful."

"Cody?" I straightened up and tested my knee. It held my weight.

She looked up at me. The crowd had grown. "Larry?" The word was softly spoken.

"I love you, Cody."

"And I love you, you big, clumsy ox."

"Talk to him, honey," a very fashionably dressed black lady said.

"Yeah," a lovely Chinese girl said. "And if you don't want him, don't toss him back. I'll take him."

I looked around. A fair-sized crowd had gathered. "What is this? Am I up for auction?"

"I'll bid," a woman said.

A roving street musician struck a few chords on the guitar and launched into song. Several of his friends, one with a fiddle and the others with banjo and accordion, joined in. The place was becoming a damn carnival.

Two young men holding hands stopped to join in the festivities. "I love her outfit," one said.

"Yes," the other said. "It's darling. But he looks like rough trade to me."

I endured the scrutiny stoically.

Cody laughed at the expression on my face.

"Kiss her, friend," said a man wearing the robes of an East Indian.

I did and the crowd went wild with applause and cheering. The musicians played louder.

A cop shoved and bullied his way through the still-growing crowd and said, "All right, all right. Break this up. What's going on here?"

A neatly dressed man carrying an expensive attaché case said, "Aw, hell, officer. They're just in love. Nothing wrong with that. We think it's nice. Come on, leave them alone."

The cop grinned. "Okay. You two carry on. More love is what this world needs."

Another round of applause went up. The crowd grew larger. More street musicians joined the impromptu band and the concert picked up in volume and spirit. The singing became louder. Traffic was all jammed up.

"You better do something before we have a dozen more cops down here," the officer said.

"Kiss him, honey!" a woman called to Cody.

She did, to the cheers of the crowd. Even the cop was smiling and applauding.

That's the City by the Bay.

I could not remember ever being in such a state of euphoria, and neither could Cody. For a time the doubts and fears that we both felt about our future vanished. We did not go out to a fancy restaurant for dinner that evening. Instead, we meandered down a side street and found a small mom and pop cafe, complete with checkered tablecloths. Just like in the movies, and it was perfect.

We ate marvelously prepared Italian food, got high on sweet table wine, and danced to old records on a jukebox that was so ancient it looked as though it could have been a carryover from the speakeasy days.

"Cody, where did you learn to slow dance? You're really very good."

"Oh," she said with a wink and a smile, "that's just one of my many hidden talents. I have so many it'll take you years to discover them all."

"I'm looking forward to those years, honey." I pulled her closer as we danced to a Hoagy Carmichael tune that had been written long before I was born. This particular rendition had been recorded back during World War Two.

"Me, too, Larry," she said with a long, contented sigh. "Me, too."

The old man and woman who ran the place smiled at us

and applauded after each dance and then gave us a couple of bottles of wine from their private stock. We had no way of knowing that the next morning, Cody and I would wish they had kept it for themselves.

We were falling-down drunk when we got back to the hotel, and both of us had the giggles. And I am definitely not the type. We giggled in the cab, while the cabbie shook his head in disbelief, finally succumbing to the infectiousness of it all and joining in. Twice he had to pull over to the curb to wipe his eyes. We were all howling at Cody's racy and totally outrageous jokes. We giggled through the lobby and all the way to the suite. Fortunately, we made it to the elevators without running into any of the religious conventioneers. Although Cody was hoping we would.

The only sound I could manage upon waking was a long, drawn-out groan.

Cody stirred beside me. "Jesus, Larry," she moaned. "What kind of wine was that?"

It took me a moment to get my thick tongue to work. "I don't know. But I'll wager it was home-brewed."

"Out of what—old tennis shoes?"

Although we had slept for a full ten hours, both of us were still somewhat intoxicated. Hell, we were still drunk. The thought of breakfast made my stomach rumble and do a slow flip-over. I groaned.

Cody slowly turned her head to look at me. "What's the matter? Other than the obvious."

"I suddenly thought of food."

She closed her eyes, sighed, and then very carefully got out of bed, walking, then running, toward the bathroom. After she finished being sick, and then showering, I did the same. We got back in bed.

"Don't get any ideas about sex," she warned me. "I don't want anything in me right now."

When we left the city late Monday afternoon, we were both silent, keeping our thoughts, though identical I'm sure, private. But they were as one: what lay ahead of us? What pitfalls were hidden in our path. Would we make a go of our new bond? Could we? Would small-town society let us? Did we have the strength to pull it off?

It was going to be a lot tougher on her. Peer pressure had never bothered me, but it was going to be a killer for Cody.

When we were airborne with our seat belts loosened, Cody said, "Larry, we'll have to be very careful—for your sake. If Vic Goodman finds out about you and me—and he will, bet on it—you'll lose your job."

"As long as I've got you, Cody, Vic doesn't worry me. There are other jobs—better ones, as a matter of fact. And where I am right now in my career, Vic's bad-mouthing can't hurt me. He's known as a prick throughout the business world. Besides, I have the money to buy my own small company—if it comes to that. And you're right, it will. So for now, don't worry your head about Vic Goodman."

"Lard-butt doesn't worry me, Larry. It's us I'm worried about. I want this to work so very badly. But I'm afraid . . ."

"Don't say it, Cody. It'll work if we try. That's all we can do."

"I guess so," she whispered.

She leaned her seat back and went to sleep. I wondered how long it would be before Vic found out about us, and what he would have to say about it.

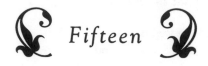 *Fifteen*

"Come on into the office, Larry," Vic ordered. "We gotta talk some, boy."

"The time has come," I muttered, pushing back my chair. Vic had been acting strangely since I'd returned from San Francisco. He had been avoiding me all week and when we did meet in the hall, we had exchanged no more than a curt nod. "Ready or not, here I come," I said, stepping out of my office.

"Watch it," my secretary warned me. "He knows about you and Cody."

That brought me up short.

"It's a small town, Mr. Baldwin. Most of us knew several weeks ago."

"I guess I've lived in the city too long," I said, smiling.

"Good luck," she said.

At his gesture, I sat down in the chair in front of Vic's desk and met him stare for stare. His gaze was not at all friendly. So he had found out about us. Big deal. It had been inevitable.

"Larry-boy," he finally said. "Do you think I'm blind or some sort of goddamn fool?"

"Get to the point, Vic." My voice was just as hard as his. Vic knew he couldn't intimidate me, and he damn sure wasn't going to jump me, so all he could do was fire me. It would have been better for all concerned had he done just that.

He remained seated behind his desk, drumming his fingers on the polished wood and staring at me. Finally, he sighed heavily and leaned back. "Larry, I built this here company up from nothin'. My daddy were a red-dirt Georgia farmer, scratchin' in the ground and a-workin' his ass off to put food on the table. Died 'fore he were fifty. I worked my tail raw to git where I am, and I didn't git here by bein' no damn fool. I warned you 'bout that trashy-assed West gal. Warned you good. But . . ."

I leaned forward. "You just take it real easy, Vic. Be very careful what you call her and how you refer to her." Something in my voice stiffened him slightly. Then he smiled and relaxed. He nodded his head.

"Well, now. Appears I'm right on the money. There shore ain't no fool like a damned old fool, Larry-boy, and you shore do take the cake there. You been struttin' 'round here a-grinnin' and actin' like the weasel that done found his way into the henhouse and now he cain't decide which chicken to gobble first."

I had put up with Vic's redneck manner for months; now I was sick of it. I leaned back in my chair. "Vic, you want to do me a very large favor?"

"What's 'at, boy?"

"Will you please knock off that goddamned, stupid-assed, corn pone-and-grits accent and speak English?"

His smile vanished and his eyes turned hard. He was silent for a time, staring at me. "All them years in the big city done made you uppity, boy. Caused you to forgit your upbringin' and made you 'shamed of your birth."

"No, Vic. I'm Georgia born and reared. But I happen to know that you can speak the English language without sounding like some ignorant cracker on his way to burn a cross in someone's yard."

His smile returned, but it was the savage smile of a predator. But Vic knew better than to pounce on me. "Why, thank you, Larry. However, there's a time and place for everything—including proper grammar." His own had suddenly improved quite dramatically. "Larry, I've known about you and the West girl for quite some time."

I didn't believe that. Had he known, he would have confronted me about it long before this. I think part of his anger was because I, or we, had fooled him for so long. But I decided to let him believe I fell for his line. "Congratulations on your network of spies, Vic, but what I do in my spare time is my concern. If my personal life ever starts to interfere with company business, I'll hand in my resignation without being asked. And you know it."

He stared at me and then nodded. "Yes. I do know that. Now, what about the girl?"

"We intend to live together."

He grunted and swore under his breath. "It's a small town, Larry. People are going to talk."

"Hell with them. Small-town gossip won't affect your business one bit. You can read stats as well as I can. You know the percentage of business from this town, as compared with . . ."

He waved me silent. "I know all that. All right, all right," he sighed. "But you have got to know how I feel . . . how I hate that little slut."

I came out of my chair in one fluid movement and it scared Vic. I could read the fear in his fat face. I put both hands on his desk and leaned over. My face was very close to his. His eyes got wide. "Vic, if you ever call her a slut again you're going to be eating your dentures. Believe it." I said it all softly, but with enough heat to convince him that I meant it.

His eyes challenged mine for only a few seconds. Then they dropped in silent surrender. I sat back down and watched him slowly nod his head. "Okay. We'll start over. You're the best I ever had working for me. I mean that. You may be the best in the business. Some folks think so. I've thought long and hard about you someday heading up this company. Larry, I'm only doing this for your own good." He held up a big hand. "I know. I know. You don't want to hear it. But you're going to hear it, and if you don't like it, then you can tell me to go to hell, we'll shake hands, then you can carry your ass and I'll be sorry to lose you. So how is it going to be?"

It was his company; he had a right to his opinion. "Okay, Vic. Speak your piece. Just don't go too far with bad-mouthing Cody. I meant what I said. I won't stand for it."

"Deal. Okay, here it is, Larry: she knows you've got big bucks. The girl is after your money."

I shook my head. "You're wrong, Vic."

"Are you telling me you didn't buy that fancy little Jap car she's driving?"

I said nothing.

He smiled. "Thought so. I couldn't prove it, though. That old man Benson, now, he hates my guts. He wouldn't tell my man a thing."

It was my turn to smile. "You must have stepped on his toes a few times, Vic. I get a strong impression that old man would cheerfully set your head on fire and stand back and laugh while it burned."

His chuckle was not at all pleasant. "Yeah, me and that old bastard have locked horns a time or two over the years. But you telling me about toe-stomping?" He grunted. "Shit, boy! You're a rogue from the git-go. So don't you get too damned high and mighty with me. Next thing you'll be telling me is you're a born-again Christian. I seen the light and praise the Lord, folks."

"Not very likely, Vic. I'll leave all that to hypocrites like you."

Vic laughed. "That's good, Larry-boy. Very good. Shows there might be some hope for you yet. Now, back to you and your . . . ah . . . teeny-bopper. She's got you all wrapped around her finger."

"I won't deny that."

"I didn't figure you would. She's pussy-whupped you, too, hey?"

I stared at him.

"I knew it. I knew it!" He slapped a hand on his desk. "There isn't another thing on God's green earth like young pussy to make a grown man go crazy. And you're living proof of that, Larry. Now drop the real bad news on me. Are you in love with her?"

"Yes."

"Goddammit, boy! I thought maybe you were just after a smooth piece of tail. Now you tell me you're in love. Love! Good God Almighty! You're old enough to be the girl's father."

"She isn't objecting." *Yet*, I added silently.

Vic leaned forward, putting his elbows on the desk, doing his best to look like good ol' Vic, every man's friend. "Larry, have you seen a doctor lately? Maybe this is a health problem. Maybe you're just going through this male menopause thing. Have you thought about that?"

"Yes. And I rejected it."

Vic sighed and muttered something under his breath. I didn't catch it and that was probably for the best.

"Why don't you just find something to fuck and forget it?" Vic suggested.

In a small way, a very small way, I felt sorry for him. "Are you all through now, Vic?"

He sighed heavily. "Yeah, I'm through. Hell, what else can I say? Get on out, Larry. Only hope I got is you'll come to your senses after that stuff starts to get old. I won't say any more about it. I don't like it. But unless or until it starts interfering with your work, it's your business. Go on back to your cun . . . girlfriend."

"So what else did the fat fart have to say?" Cody asked.

I was helping her unpack her clothes, and taking note that she didn't have that many things. She had had a rougher time of it than I first suspected, but she had never complained. At least not to my knowledge. She just wasn't the type.

"Nothing of any real importance. Cody, I spoke with Tom today. Your parents put the house where your aunt lived in your name. Did you know about that?"

She looked up, surprise in her eyes. "No. This is the first I've heard of it. Why would they do that?"

"Several reasons. First, to provide some security for you. And secondly, they obviously knew about your aunt's deteriorating condition and this way the state can't take the house to sell it to provide care for her."

"I thought the house belonged to Aunt Blanche."

"Obviously not."

"Who's been paying for the insurance?"

"Tom said part of the insurance money you received was set aside for that purpose. Do you want to sell the house?"

"No. Not just yet, Larry."

"Okay. When you see Tom, tell him. He's handling everything."

She nodded. "I can't believe old fatso didn't fire you."

"He's not going to kill the goose that lays the golden egg, Cody. I make too much money for the Goodman Company. But I suggest we don't push our luck by moving into the company house."

"Oh, no way. I like it right here. That other place is just too damn big."

"Have you talked to any of your friends about us?" I tossed the question out casually.

"A few."

"And?"

She shrugged and changed the subject. I had met a few of her friends and the feeling was mutual: they didn't like me and I didn't like them. Her friends—few though they were—were just going to be another barrier. Seemed like if it wasn't Vic, it was Cody's friends. And I knew only too well how the young value friends and also how intolerant the young can be . . . just as intolerant as the older folks. Or more so.

With both of us working full-time jobs, we soon settled into what I thought was a comfortable routine. On Friday or Saturday nights we would drive into Atlanta for dinner and a movie. We did not socialize with others. I only knew a few people in Pine Hills and Cody flatly refused to go anywhere near the country club. She liked movies so I bought a satellite system and subscribed to everything. I think we had about a hundred and fifty different channels to choose from.

I thought things were going well, and for a time, they were. True to his word, after our talk in his office, Vic never brought up the subject of Cody again.

But others did.

"The folks of Pine Hills are having a real good time gossiping about us, Larry," Cody said over dinner one evening.

"Did you think they wouldn't?"

"Why can't people just mind their own business?"

"That goes against human nature, honey. What are they saying?"

She shrugged as she picked at her food. "Just the usual crap, I suppose. Cody West shacked up with a monied man. Cody is a golddigger. Cody is no good. They've always liked to gossip about me; this is just more grist for the mill. I can take it."

"You want to move, Cody?"

She looked up from her plate. "Move?"

"Yes. I'm looking at a small company in the Midwest. Kansas City area. We could make a brand new start."

"You'd do that for me?"

"For you, for me, for us."

"It's something to think about."

She might have thought about it, but if she did she never mentioned it to me.

The short time fate allowed us together was the happiest of my life. Now, looking back, and looking back is all I can do, I am absolutely certain of that.

We had our spats, but they were usually over the silliest things. And the making-up was delightful.

At night, I usually read while she watched movies. They definitely were not my kind of entertainment. I grew up on Cooper, Bogart, Gable, Bergman, Hepburn, and the like.

"How can you watch that crap?" I finally asked one evening.

"It's funny," she replied, surprised at my question.

"About as funny as an iron lung."

"Well, excuse me," she said, getting up and clicking off the TV. "I think I'll go for a drive."

I should have seen it happening. I should have seen it beginning to unravel. But the spats were over what I thought were very minor things. Minor to me, but not to her. I just didn't see the wedge that was slowly and irrevocably being driven between us.

At age twenty-two, I was mature and fighting a dirty and savage little secret war. I think I was a grown man, both mentally and physically, long before that.

The spats notwithstanding, I did become a great many things to Cody over the few months that we lived together: the father she lost while a teenager, the big brother she never had, lover, and confidant. I worried about the advice I gave her—when she did occasionally ask for my opinion. And those times were getting fewer and fewer—I failed to pick up on that, too. Until it was too late.

On the plus side of our relationship, we were both, for the most part, stay-at-home types. We liked to go to bed early and get up early. We were both voracious readers, and despite her total lack of taste in movies and music, Cody constantly surprised me with her knowledge of authors who had hit their peak long before she'd been born.

"So I like Steinbeck," she said when I complimented her on her choice of reading matter. "Sue me." She smiled and winked. "I also like Meat Loaf."

"Well, fix it for supper, then."

She sighed and rolled her eyes. "Forget it, Larry. We're on different wave lengths."

I didn't realize at the time just how much truth was in those words.

There were a lot of things I didn't grasp until it was too late—the most important being that love alone cannot sustain a relationship.

I also learned about Cody's moods, some of them quite mercurial. At times I thought her to be a fatalist, for she firmly believed that something terrible and tragic was going to happen to her while she was young.

It did.

I suppose, in retrospect, I was going through the infatuation I should have discovered as a teenager, but did not, and the true, deep love I should have experienced as an adult, but had not.

I finally got it through my head that Cody was missing her own age group, so I suggested she have some of her friends out for drinks and steaks.

Bad mistake.

The evening was a big flop, although, to give myself some credit, I did try very hard to get with the program. But I did not speak their language or share their mostly liberal and very narrow values. The generation gap was too wide, and we had absolutely nothing in common. Her friends didn't really like or trust me; I was an adult, and they were still reaching for adulthood. And I could not help but recall that when I was their age, I had already undergone some of the most brutal training ever devised by man and was fighting a guerrilla war.

Most of her male friends seemed to have a great deal of difficulty removing the cap from a bottle of beer. I recalled with a secret sigh that I'd once used a broken beer bottle to kill a man.

But I did try to break through to her friends that evening. Lord, how I tried.

"You didn't try hard enough, Larry," she said as we prepared for bed.

"What the hell did you want me to do, Cody? Their politics suck. They don't know anything about the real world. They want something for nothing. They think the government owes them a living. They . . ."

"And you think you know all the answers, huh?" she said, abruptly cutting me off.

"Not all of them, Cody. But enough of them to know that your friends are full of shit."

She slept on the couch that night.

The strain on our emotional screws began to really tighten after that, and Cody began spending some afternoons after work at a friend's house. I couldn't and didn't blame her.

The talk around town was fierce, and she took a hell of a lot of flak from her peer group . . . her so-called friends. She kept most of that from me—I didn't learn of it until long after everything had fallen apart.

We really began to lose ground when the company she worked for shut its doors and locked up the local factory. I had known the closing was in the works, and maybe I should have tried to prepare her. I just didn't think it would make that much difference. I had plenty of money and thought she would like to stay home for a time. Again, I was wrong.

I tried to apologize but she wasn't having any. She had changed right before my eyes, becoming moody, irritable, flaring up at the smallest thing, lashing out at me.

"Cody, what in the hell is wrong with you?"

I got the silent treatment. Really pissed me off. I stormed out of the house and went for a drive to cool off. She was better when I returned, almost civil, but there was very definitely a wall growing between us and I couldn't figure out who had laid the first brick.

We quarreled just before I had to go on the road for a few days that turned into several weeks. It was, as usual, a quarrel over nothing. But I left angry. Bad thing to do. But Cody had been acting childish for several weeks, and I said some things that shouldn't have been said.

"Cody, why don't you grow up?" I asked her right before I left.

She leveled those eyes at me. "Maybe I have, Larry. Maybe that's it."

"Now what does that mean?"

She turned her back to me, refusing to reply.

"I'll call you every night I'm gone, Cody."

She turned around to face me. "Larry, I'm . . ." She shook her head.

I waited. "You're what, Cody?"

"It isn't important. I'll . . . see you, Larry."

"Cody. Let's don't part like this. Tell me what's been bothering you."

"Like I said, it isn't important."

She walked into the bedroom.

"Shit!" I said, and walked out the door.

I had been on the road for several days before I worked off my anger, put pride aside, and called her . . . or attempted to. But when no one answered the phone, I knew the slender thread was fraying. I tried our place in the country and her house in town. I called both places a dozen times a day. I got the answering machine at the country house and the phone in town was never picked up. But I couldn't cut my trip short, for I was working on a million-dollar deal and it had to be closed as quickly as possible.

Cody would just have to understand how it was. She wasn't a kid; she was a grown woman. I had tried to explain big business to her many times, about how easily contracts could be won or lost in this highly competitive world. Maybe I didn't try hard enough; maybe she just couldn't understand. I don't know. All I could do was put the unanswered calls out of my mind and carry on with business as usual.

Biggest mistake of my life.

After three weeks on the road, I finally touched down in Atlanta. I made my report to Vic and handed him the signed contracts. I could practically see the dollar signs light up in his eyes.

I drove out to our house and discovered why Cody had not answered my calls. The answering machine tape was full of my one-sided calls.

The small house was empty.

Cody was gone.

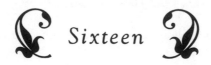 Sixteen

I walked through the silent house, filled with so many memories. In the bedroom, I noticed a few of her things were still there . . . all the clothes and shoes I had bought for her in San Francisco. Her "fancy clothes," as she called them. Then I saw the note propped up on the dresser, written in her small, neat handwriting.

I really didn't want to read it, for I had a pretty good hunch what it was going to say. In the service we used to call them "Dear John" letters.

I sat on the edge of the bed for several minutes, just looking at the note, before I worked up the courage to read it. I was right. Dear John, I sent your saddle home.

> Larry,
>
> After you left, I spent a couple of nights at my house in town, then I came back out here. I waited for you to call all afternoon and most of the evening. Then I got tired of waiting. Guess you had a lot to do.

I understand. Job, and all. I understand a lot of things now. So I just packed my things and left. I'm going to Atlanta to stay for a while. I've got to try to get it all together. I really have to decide about some things. But I have made up my mind that I can't continue living with you, and I can't marry you. I'm not going to sponge off of you. So do us both a favor and leave me alone for a time. Let me get my head straight.

I warned you, Larry. I warned you when we began all this that it probably wouldn't work, even though I do love you and I know you love me.

I have a lot of thinking to do.

Cody

I folded the note and put it in my jacket pocket. I sat on the bed for a time, too stunned to move. Maybe I was even in mild shock. I cussed myself for not being here when Cody needed someone to lean on. I cussed myself for not being more understanding. But goddammit, I had a job to do—and I was doing it for both of us. I still had no clue as to why she was so upset. Then I remembered how evasive she'd become about a week before I left. And how moody and depressed.

After a shower and a shave, I headed for Atlanta. I had a hunch where to find her.

It was eight o'clock when I entered the singles joint. Nothing had changed. Cody was sitting at the bar, looking very alone, very sad, and heartbreakingly lovely. I walked over and took the stool next to her. I waited for her to open the conversation.

Without looking up from her drink, she sighed and said, "I smell a very familiar and very expensive cologne. So it has to be good ol' Larry Baldwin."

"That's me."

"How you doin', lover?"

"Not too good, Cody-kid. When I got back to the nest, it was empty."

"Yeah, I know. I got tired of trying to keep it patched up with twigs and leaves. Sorry about that."

"It was all business, Cody. It wasn't another woman."

"I know that, Larry. It isn't another man with me."

She still had not looked at me.

"Cody . . ."

"I thought I asked you to leave me alone, Larry."

"If you had really meant that, Cody, you wouldn't be in this bar. But if you want me to leave, just say so and I'll go away."

She slowly shook her head and sighed heavily, as if she was carrying the weight of Atlanta on her slender shoulders. "I guess we have to talk—I know we do—but I've really been dreading it. It'll be rough on both of us."

I played a long shot. "Cody, do you want to come back home and talk there?"

"No," she said firmly. "That's out. Period. Larry, let's not make this any more difficult than it already is. I hurt enough for a dozen people."

The bartender finally got off his ass and strolled our way. I waved him back. Waiting until he was out of earshot, I said, "Cody, I don't know what I've done to upset you."

She turned to look at me. With a sigh, she said, "It isn't you, Larry. It's me."

"You want to explain that?"

She nodded, one lock of hair falling over an eye. I resisted an impulse to brush it back. "One of the times you were away, some of my friends dropped by, wanting me to go party with them. They don't like to come out while you're there. They, well, they don't feel right. They don't feel comfortable around you, Larry. They get tense."

"Thanks a lot. Is it my aftershave or deodorant?"

"Oh, Larry." She put a soft hand on mine. "It's not just the age difference. That could be overcome. You're L. J. Baldwin, star football player in college, who turned his back on a professional career worth a lot of money. They don't understand that. You're an ex-Green Beret type with lots of medals. God and country and all that stuff. Larry, they know you can cripple and kill with your bare hands. They're scared of you. You have a . . . well, a presence about you. A bearing. You're ramrod straight. You're a big shot in business—a man who makes more money than my friends can even imagine. You don't like their lifestyle, you don't like their music, you don't like their movies . . ." She shook her head. "Oh, hell, I'm not saying any of this right. All those things I just said, that's part of the reason I love you."

I had to think about that for a moment. "Now I am confused. Go on, Cody, let it out. Get it all said and out in the open."

About that time the music—loosely speaking—cranked up, the deejay screaming some incomprehensible message. I tossed some bills on the bar and took Cody's arm, leading her out of the joint.

And as we had done before, only a precious few months and a thousand memories ago, we walked out into the summer-warm night and went back to that same little cafe. Only the waitress had changed. We took the same table by the window. Coffee for me, soft drink for her.

"You hungry, Cody?"

She shook her head.

"You feel all right?"

"Oh, I'm okay. I just don't have much of an appetite." She smiled at me. "I could stand to lose a few pounds anyway."

"Yeah, sure," I replied, returning the smile.

"I really thought we had a chance, Larry," she said, her eyes not meeting mine. "I really did. But . . ." She shrugged. "It doesn't matter now." Her eyes lifted, touching mine. I knew what was coming and felt sick at my stomach. She sighed again, almost a painful sound. "That person who wrote the line about May-September romances was right, Larry. At least for us. So let's just quit before the hurt gets too bad."

She wasn't telling me everything. I was very good at picking up nuances, and I knew she was holding back on me. But I couldn't imagine why. She was contradicting herself. I knew she had told her friends to butt out. And I didn't buy that bit about her male friends being afraid of me. Not for a second. Something was all fouled up here, but it was obvious she was not going to level with me.

I touched her hand. "I love you, Cody."

She squeezed my hand gently. "And I love you, Larry. Too much, I guess." Tears were forming in her eyes, misting the blue. "A part of me will always love you," she whispered. "You just don't understand and I can't tell you. It wouldn't be fair."

"You mean you won't tell me and it wouldn't be fair to whom?"

"It wouldn't be fair to either one of us."

"We could still see each other, Cody. We could try to work this thing out."

The tears sprang freely now, slowly tracing sad silver paths down her cheeks. "Larry, that would . . . only make matters worse." Her voice was almost a sob. "It's got to end. And it's got to end right now. I just don't have a choice in the matter. Don't press me for more than that. I'm begging you. Please?"

"I have to press you, Cody. Because I don't understand any of this. What is it you're not telling me, and why?"

"Nothing!" she cried softly.

But the word fell flat. She was lying, and Cody never could lie worth a damn.

"Larry, believe this if you never believe anything else. I do love you. But it's got to end tonight. I love you with all my heart. Believe that. But don't ask me to explain why this just has to be. Please? I beg you, don't."

So there was a lot more to it, and she wasn't going to tell me. But I would respect her wishes. I nodded my head. I didn't push the issue. It was over. We sat in silence for a time, just looking at each other. Finally, I said, "Are you staying in the city tonight?"

She did not trust her voice. She nodded and the tears spilled out, falling on the tabletop.

"Where is your car?"

"Down the street," she managed to say. She was openly sobbing and my heart was breaking.

"You take a few minutes to get yourself together, then I'll walk you to your car."

"All right," she whispered.

I left money on the table and started to leave. Then I turned around and picked that up, replacing it with a twenty-dollar bill, just as I'd done before . . . when love was just beginning to blossom. Taking Cody's arm, we walked out of the cafe. That was one place that would never see me again.

We said nothing as we walked to her car. A very fine, light mist had begun falling, slicking the street. We could hear the music from the singles joint. I wondered how nearby apartment dwellers tolerated it. Cody angled me across the street to her car.

I broke the silence. "I'll send you a clear title to the car, Cody, and have Tom set up a checking account at my bank for you until you can find another job and get settled in."

"Larry . . ."

"No," I shushed her. "I want to do that. I know a fellow here in the city—department head of a small company. I'll call him and see what I can do about finding you a job. I'll leave the number with Tom. You check in with him in a few days. I want to do these last few things. Cody, please get your things out of the house this weekend—okay?"

She shook her head. "Those clothes I left were the ones you bought me, Larry. They're just too fancy for me. I don't need them. I don't want them."

"Whatever you say, Cody."

She put her arms around me and pressed close. She stayed there for a long time and I was glad to hold her.

Cody lifted her face. "Kiss for luck, Dads?" She asked it with a smile, but the tears were streaming down her cheeks.

"I wouldn't have it any other way, Cody-kid."

When she kissed me, her tears were hot on my lips. And I'll remember that kiss all the rest of my life. The fine mist falling from the sky wet the city's streets; it touched her hair, creating tiny, glistening beads of diamond-like light.

I tried a smile that almost made it, then touched her face with my fingertips. Very gently. "Goodbye, Cody."

She tried to speak, then broke down, the tears rushing in twin rivers. "Oh, God!" she managed to say, then pulled away from me and went running to her car.

I stood on the sidewalk for a time, waiting for her to crank her car and pull out. When the taillights had faded, I drove to a small, very expensive, and very adult piano bar and ordered a drink. A double. I smiled ruefully and dropped a ten-dollar bill into the huge snifter on the bar.

The piano player smiled at me. "You got a request?"

Cody's face flashed before my eyes. "Yeah," I said with a sigh. "How about 'The Shadow of Your Smile'?"

"That's a good one." He rippled the keys. "But judging from the expression on your face when you walked in, I might have thought more along the lines of 'One For My Baby and One More For the Road.'"

"That's a good one, too." I dropped another ten spot in the snifter.

"Naw," he said. "You're too young to remember that one."

"I'm over forty."

"I got a couple more to do before yours, okay?"

"Sure."

He began playing "Stranger On the Shore" and I said, "That's another good one for this evening."

He smiled. "You and your lady have a fuss?"

I took a sip of Crown Royal over ice. Love on the rocks. "Yeah," I told him. "For a fact."

When he started playing the theme from *Love Story*, I just about lost it. I managed to sit through my requests, nodded in appreciation, and left. When I walked out the door, he was playing "Who Can I Turn To?"

I stayed at the company house all day Saturday and most of Sunday, never leaving, in case Cody did return to the country place for something. I watched a lot of TV and couldn't tell you what I'd watched five minutes after the program was over. Late Sunday, I drove back to the country. Every room seemed to be filled with her; the house seemed to share my sadness as I felt the emptiness of every corner of every room.

I had stopped at a supermarket in town and picked up some boxes, and began quickly packing up all the clothes she had left behind. That was not something I ever want to do again. It just about did me in—the scent of her lingered on every garment, and lingered on my hands long afterward.

On the table in the den lay a sheet of white notebook paper. So Cody had driven out for one last look. I thought she might. I sat down and looked at the paper. She had drawn a picture of a butterfly, all done in reds and blacks and blues. It was beautiful and I still have it. I had it framed. She had written a small verse under the colorful drawing:

Butterflies fly lonely
Fly high
But they are free to
Fly.
High away, far away.
Lonely.
I love you, Larry.
Goodbye.

I packed up my gear and locked up the house, then headed back to town.

It was just as lonely as the house in the country.

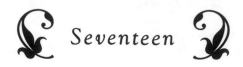

Seventeen

Monday, after checking in at the office and clearing my desk of papers to be signed and letters to be dictated and orders to be okayed, I called Tom Vanderwedge for an appointment . . . all the while knowing I was on his shit-list. At first, his secretary wouldn't even put me through. I told her I'd come down there in person and create a very nasty scene if I didn't get to speak with him. Tom finally came on the line and granted me an appointment.

I had him send Cody a clear title to the car and paid up her insurance as far as I could. Then I gave him money to deposit in her account.

Tom had known all along that Cody and I had been living together, and I knew he had not approved. But he did as I requested, then told me, "I don't want your business after this, Mr. Baldwin. Find yourself another attorney."

"You will do this for me, though?"

"Only for Cody's sake. Hell with you!"

No doubt about it: the barrister was a gutsy little bastard. I nodded and left his office and his accusing eyes. He refused to shake my hand. I didn't blame him.

Vic never made any reference to my sudden increase of time spent at the office, but he seemed happier and patted me on the back every now and then, inviting me to his office for working lunches and for drinks out at the club—like we used to do.

Before Cody.

And that was the way I viewed it: Before Cody and After Cody. With a very sharp knife, an invisible blade, I surgically attempted to excise about six months of my life. But the operation was not a success. The patient lived. I couldn't cut deep enough into my soul to remove that intangible called love. I had successfully eluded that feeling for forty-one years, side-stepping every time it pecked on the door of my heart. But ol' Larry had to wait until middle age before laying out the welcome mat.

Now the goddamn door wouldn't close.

I would just have to live with it.

Somehow.

I called my friend in Atlanta and got Cody an appointment to see him about a job. Naturally, she got it. All she had to do was smile one time.

I did my best to avoid the places where I might run into her, but in a small town, that's next to impossible. I saw her several times during the next few weeks. She would wave and smile. I would ignore her. Finally she got the message and our chance encounters deteriorated into stony, silent looks of accusation and hurt.

Sure, she was hurting—much more than I knew at the time—and trying to make the best of a bad situation. I tried hard to hate Cody. I'd always heard that there's a fine line between love and hate. I discovered that with me it was about as wide as the Grand Canyon and I soon gave up trying to hate her. That was impossible. At home, listening to Verdi's *Rigoletto*, I tried to adapt my thinking to that of the Duke of Mantua and the scorn he felt for women. "Feathers in the wind," he called them—fickle, lacking the ability to tell the truth.

I failed there, as well.

In searching my memory, I could not remember a single time when Cody had lied. Indeed, the lying had come only from my lips, not hers.

I dreaded the time—and I felt sure it would surely come—when I would see her out on a date. So I didn't go out much at night. Instead, my nights were whiskey-filled, ending with me in an alcohol-induced stupor on the couch, dreaming of Cody.

Fortunately, none of that carried over into my work. If anything, my performance improved—I was driving myself harder than ever before, and the sales picture at the Goodman Company reflected my hard work. He was, in his quaint way of putting it, "Jist as proud as punch, Larry-boy. Yes, sirree, bob. You got ol' Vic a-grinnin' lak a big coon with a watermelon."

He was not referring to the four-legged animal.

I could make it through the work days, from early in the morning until after dark. Hard, driving work, exhausting work, so I could sleep at night—with the help of a bottle of booze. But even with all that, many of the nights were killers. When I did sleep, my dreams were of Cody, and always, in the background, that strange scene was replayed: the flashing lights and the crying of women, the wailing of sirens. Vic standing in the dream-induced fog, holding something and pointing and laughing. The damn dream was never clearly in focus. I didn't know why he was laughing or what he was pointing at. The dream would leave me depressed and tired upon awakening.

Finally, while on a business trip to the Big Apple, I called a woman I'd known for years. In plain terms, Carmen ran a stable of whores. Escorts. All college-educated and multi-lingual. I told Carmen I wanted to talk. I was pretty screwed up.

Carmen knew me; I had used her escort services for reluctant clients many times in the past, and we had discovered that we genuinely liked each other. "Woman troubles, Larry? I can't believe it. I guess you're human after all. Sorry. Forgive me. I had no right to say that."

"But it's true, Carmen," I admitted. "Hard-ass Larry Baldwin finally got his long overdue comeuppance."

"Larry, I have a suggestion: would you settle for an evening with a slightly over-the-hill madam? All on the house. I owe you."

"Are you serious, Carmen? I can't think of another person I'd rather spend the evening with."

She laughed mockingly. "You're lying, Larry."

"Oh?"

"Yes. You'd much rather be spending it with the woman who has you all tied up in knots."

No one knew how old Carmen was—except that she was well past forty. But she sure wasn't over the hill by any means. She was probably one of the most beautiful women in the city—for her age. She was tall and willowy, with light brown hair streaked carefully with gray. Her figure was fantastic, and she kept in shape. Carmen probably knew more about the male libido than a whole room full of shrinks. But no shrink would dare charge what she did for a session.

She picked me up at the hotel, took one look, and hustled me off to her masseuse. "You look like death warmed over, Larry," she said bluntly. "How much booze have you been drinking a night and for how long?"

I told her.

"Jesus Christ! Are you eating?"

"Oh, yeah. I've been eating. When I remember."

"Well, I can fix you up. What you need is a good long steam and rubdown, and a shoulder to cry on." She smiled. "And maybe some time in bed."

"Carmen, I'll be honest: I don't even know if I could get it up. Or if I want to."

She chuckled. "If I want it up, Larry, I'll get it up, don't you worry."

She wasn't boasting—just stating a fact. And giving me quite a compliment as well. Carmen had quit hustling years back. I knew part of the story. She had been pushed into whoring by her father when she was about twelve. He had raped her when she was ten or so. She ran away from him at age thirteen, hopped a bus out of Miami, and had not been back.

But Carmen, like her stable of girls, was not your run-of-the-mill hooker. She had made a fortune, earned a degree from CCNY, and opened her own modeling and talent agency. She was a very wealthy woman and had never, to my knowledge, been married. A well-known pimp in the city had tried, years back, to move in on her. Carmen shot him right between the eyes and had the corpse fitted with concrete shoes and dumped in the East River. The rumor was that even the mob left her alone.

She told her masseuse to work me over until I hollered, and then do it again. And the lady did just that, following orders to the letter. I thought I was going to die. But when she finished, I knew Carmen had been right: it was what I needed.

We had dinner at a restaurant that practically takes an act of Congress to get in. But Carmen breezed us right past the maitre d' as if she owned the place. Turned out she did.

"Not bad for a gal who started out selling her ass for five bucks a throw to bums and drunks, hey, Larry?" She said it with a hard smile.

She had called in our order while I was being pureed, pounded, and parboiled. The meal was delicious, making me realize that although I had been eating over the past few weeks, I had been concentrating more on drinking.

Back at her apartment, she made a pot of coffee and then coaxed the story out of me. I told it all, leaving nothing out: the scheming, the lies, and the love. When I finished, she shook her head—whether in disgust or empathy, I didn't know.

She poured us more coffee and sat down. "You poor dumb bastard. Falling in love with a kid."

I felt a strong urge to defend Cody and opened my mouth to do so, then closed it.

Carmen smiled. "Go ahead, Larry. Tell me all about how mature she is for her age, and about all her other fine qualities. Tell me how intelligent she is. That's what you were about to do, isn't it?"

Like I said: one smart lady. "Yeah, I was, Carmen. But what would be the point?"

She stared at me for a moment. "Have you cried yet, Larry?"

The question startled me. I shook my head. "Don't be ridiculous, Carmen. I haven't cried since I was nine . . . no, eight."

Again, that knowing smile. "Oh, right. How silly of me. Men don't cry, do they, Larry?" She laughed bitterly. "You really are in love with the young lady, aren't you? I thought at first you were just in love with love, but this is the genuine article, isn't it?"

I nodded. "Damn sure is."

"Had you ever been in love before, Larry?"

"No. Never."

"Jesus. You really got a double shot, didn't you?" Before I could reply, she said, "It's a miserable feeling, isn't it, baby?"

I turned my head and looked at her, unspoken questions leaping from my eyes.

She picked up on it. "Oh, yes, dear. I've been in love. Whores fall in love, too, you know. We may be whores—albeit high-class—but we're still women."

"Are you . . ." I allowed my question to slip off into emptiness.

"Still in love with him? Do you really want me to answer that truthfully, Larry?"

"Yes."

"I haven't seen the man in ten years and I'm as much in love with him right now as I was then."

"Ten fucking years!" I blurted. "Oh, come on, Carmen. That's only in the movies."

She shook her head and smiled sadly and knowingly. "Don't you believe it, Larry. But it's not as bad as it sounds," she tried to reassure me. "The memory fades after a time. Some days you won't be able to put a face to the person. It'll turn into a memory that you just can't quite shake, that's all. A vague mental haunting that's always in the back of your mind, that pops up to confront you at the damnedest times. Just when you're about to make it with someone you think is special—bang!—there it is. You learn to live with it, Larry. You have to," she added gently. "You learn to live with the feelings it sets off, and you learn to avoid those things that trigger it: a certain type of clothing, a certain perfume—in my case, cologne—the same kind you use, by the way. The next time you come up here, change brands. Give my memories a break."

I chuckled; first time I'd done that in weeks. "I'll remember, Carmen."

"You'll be strolling along and see a person with the same hairstyle or mannerism, the same walk, and it'll all come rushing back. Pray you never see her again, Larry. If you do, everything you once felt will come back and hit you right in the face and you're back to ground zero."

I was silent for a moment, then glanced at her. "I'll beat this, Carmen."

She shook her head and her smile was sad. "No, you won't, baby. Not if it was true love. You'll just learn to live with it. But let me tell you something—words of wisdom from an old whore: I'm glad I fell in love." She read my expression of surprise. "Yes. Really. You'd be surprised at the number of people who never experience it, who go through their entire lives without knowing what it is to fall in love, who confuse passion with love. Or attach something dirty to it. True love isn't dirty. It's wonderful.

"For all the hurt that love can bring, Larry—wasn't it glorious while it was in full bloom? Wasn't every second you spent together precious? You know it was. And right now, though you're hurting more than you ever thought you possibly could, you wouldn't trade those memories for anything in the world. Would you, Larry?"

Again, I chuckled. I had to admit she was right. "No, Carmen. I wouldn't."

She gathered up our coffee cups and stacked them on the sink of the wet bar. Leaning against it, she said, "Go on back to your hotel, Larry. Wallow in your memories awhile longer. You're pretty much over the hard drinking now—and far too smart to kill yourself with booze. You're like me: we both love money too much to let anything interfere with making it for long. No, Larry, you don't want just any woman tonight—only the woman you can't have. It wouldn't be good for either of us."

I stood up and got my jacket. "You're a wise woman, Carmen. Maybe you should hang a shingle outside your door."

She got a good laugh out of that—a throaty, lusty laugh. "Larry, when you get it all back together, come see me. I've always wanted to know how you are in bed."

That brought another smile to my lips. "Well, Carmen, I've been told I'm pretty good."

She matched my smile. "Me, too, baby. Me, too."

The weeks rolled slowly by and hot summer held sway. I suppose I was getting better, or just learning to live without Cody. I wasn't drinking nearly as much, but I was having some difficulty sleeping. Several nights a week I resorted to drugs, the sleeping pills pulling me down into a restless slumber. The arms of Morpheus were not gentle arms for me.

I continued to have that same strange nightmare, over and over. Something about it troubled me deeply. It was almost like an evil omen.

Disturbing talk about Cody had reached me: the crowd she was running with, the things they were doing. I hoped it was all just talk. I knew if I heard the rumors, so would Vic, and he did.

"Larry," he said after closing the door and plopping down into a chair in my office. "Let's you and me talk some. Man to man."

"All right, Vic. Want some coffee?"

"No, no. My eyeballs is floatin' now. Larry, I know you done dropped that Cody West gal, and I'm proud as hell about you comin' to your senses. I knew you had it in you. Now then, you 'bout to git your life all in order?"

The last thing in this world or the next I wanted was to discuss my personal life—and Cody—with this pig-eyed, meddling fart. But I nodded. "Yes, Vic. It's all back in order. Why do you ask?"

"Well, hell's fire, boy! Lord love a duck!" We were back in the barnyard, slopping hogs again. "'Cause I'm concerned 'bout you, that's why."

I kept my smile hidden. Ol' Vic would drop his upper plate when I got around to telling him I was negotiating to buy the controlling interest in a large office supply company head-quartered in the Midwest.

Vic wriggled around in the chair. "You know that Cody-girl done got herself fired from her job in the city, don't you?" He could scarcely conceal his glee.

"No, Vic. I didn't. What happened?"

"Well, 'way I heared it, she took to squallin' 'bout half the time; couldn't keep her mind on her work. Drugs, I betcha. Some of these young people nowadays, Larry, they jist can't leave them old pills and shit-dope alone, you know? I reckon she's one of them. I just can't 'magine nothin' like it—her all of a sudden to commence to start squallin' and bawlin' right out in public, at work. I bet that's a sight to see."

I bet it was, too. But why would Cody do that? Was she ill?

Vic rambled on for another minute or so about young people in general and Cody in particular, but he was careful not to call her bad names. I could tell he wanted to ask me a lot of questions, but didn't quite know how to start or how far he could safely push the issue. I was grateful when my secretary buzzed the intercom, telling me that Mr. Goodman had people waiting to see him in his office. I was very happy when he left; happier still to flip him the bird as he closed the door behind him.

"Up yours, Vic," I muttered.

I cleared my desk of paperwork and left the office early that Friday. Vic had already left for the day. I was both puzzled and concerned about Cody. Why would she suddenly start crying at work? She was just not that type. In many ways she was a very private person.

I drove past Cody's house. Her car was not parked in the drive. I drove through town, looking for her in vain.

When I got home, I tried to call her. Her number had been changed. Unlisted.

"Shit!" I said, slamming down the receiver.

I was sure Tom Vanderwedge had her new number, and was equally certain he wouldn't give it to me. Tom wouldn't even speak to me on the street.

Once more, I drove over to her house and this time I got out of the car and knocked on the door. If she was home, and I didn't believe she was, she wasn't answering the door.

I drove around town until dusk without spotting her. Maybe she had gone into the city for the weekend.

I thought about heading into Atlanta and checking out that singles joint, then thought better of it. If I knew anything at all about Cody, and I did, that would be the last place she would ever return to. Too many bad memories.

I finally gave up the search and went home. Over the next few hours, I fixed a couple of drinks and paced the floor until I damn near wore myself out. I finally said to hell with it and took a sleeping pill and went to bed, waiting for that strange nightmare to grip me.

It was much more vivid than ever before and the scene itself had changed. Now the sounds of grinding metal were

added to the din. I was in a huge building of some sort. Cobwebs and dust and broken objects . . . and screaming. Wild screaming over and over.

Finally the nightmare faded and I slept.

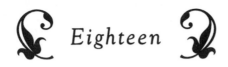 Eighteen

I stilled the ringing phone. "Larry!" Tom Vanderwedge's angry voice jarred me out of a dull sleep. "Goddammit, Larry, wake up."

"I'm awake. I'm up," I said, glancing at the clock-radio on the nightstand. Five o'clock. Still dark. "What the hell is wrong, Tom?"

"Get your ass out of bed and get over to that old warehouse out on the edge of town. Where all that old construction equipment is stored."

"Warehouse? Construction equipment?" My mind was still fuzzy from the sleeping pill. What the hell was he shouting about?

"Goddammit, Larry!" Tom yelled.

"Tom, are you drunk? What the hell's the problem? Jesus, it's still dark out."

Then it hit me. My dream last night had been inside an old warehouse. Jesus God! I felt cold and sick at my stomach as I put the phone on speaker and started scrambling into my clothes.

"Talk to me, Tom. I'm getting dressed. What happened? Where are you?"

"I'm on my car phone out at the warehouse. It's Cody, Larry. I can't prove any of this, but Mike Goodman and several of his friends somehow got Cody and two of her girl-friends—they'd been riding around in Cody's car—to that warehouse. The girls were beaten and raped, Larry. At least Cody was. The boys are claiming the girls consented to it all. Cody managed to get away and Mike went after her in that goddamn huge truck of his. He rammed her car. She's pinned in and hurt . . . I don't know how badly. Get over here, Larry. I've just discovered some things you should know. And Cody wants to talk to you. I'm just hitting the high spots. I'll explain in full when you get here."

I sat down on the edge of the bed to pull on my socks and shoes. He'd discovered some things? "What things, Tom?"

"Get over here, goddammit!" he screamed, then broke the connection.

"On my way," I muttered, buttoning up my shirt and heading for the front door.

Quite a crowd had gathered both outside and inside of the old chain link fence that surrounded the warehouse and all the junked equipment. The police and sheriff's deputies were having a hard time with crowd control. Portable floodlights had been set up around the two vehicles: Mike's huge truck and Cody's little car. The truck had suffered little damage, but Cody's car was horse-shoed . . . and she was pinned inside.

My nightmarish premonition finally began to make sense. The warehouse, the junked equipment. Vic had driven past the site the same day I'd seen Cody for the first time, coming out of the dress shop. Vic had said the warehouse should be torn down and the equipment hauled away. Said somebody was going to get hurt out here someday. Kids liked to come out to the site and park and make out and smoke dope. There were gaping holes all over the chain-link fence.

So maybe that was the reason I kept dreaming about it—I was associating it with the first time I'd seen Cody. That was the best I could come up with.

And there was Vic, his arm around Mike, pointing at the wrecked vehicles and shouting.

"Where the hell is the highway patrol with the Jaws?" a cop yelled, referring to the Jaws of Life, a device that slices through metal.

For the moment, the police weren't allowing anyone close to where Cody was pinned. But I intended to go over there, one way or the other.

Tom came to my side. "The word is, Larry, that Vic Goodman held you over Cody's head. He told her that if she didn't break off the relationship, he'd have her aunt kicked out of the nursing home and put out into the street."

"Hell, he can't do that!"

"He owns the nursing home, Larry. He owns a whole string of them in this part of the state."

"That son of a bitch." I tried to step around Tom to go to Cody but the lawyer grabbed my arm. "Vic also sent some muscle around to see Cody. They were pretty graphic about what they would do to her if she didn't leave you. I can't prove any of this, Larry, but it comes from good sources. And it fits."

"Cody . . ."

"Is alive, Larry. She's got some broken bones and possibly some internal injuries. But she's alive. You try to go over there and the cops will arrest you."

"Oh, I'm going to Cody, Tom. Bet on that. One way or the other."

Chief Pardue and several of his patrolmen were standing close to Vic and Mike. Vic had an arm around his son's shoulders, patting him, holding him, just like in the dream. The punk looked pleased. Vic threw me an angry look. It did not compare with the look I gave him. Several EMTs and county deputies were surrounding Cody's car, the scene bathed in harsh light from the portable floods. I could not see Cody. I shrugged off Tom's hand and walked over to Vic.

"I tole you to stay away from that slut, Larry," Vic said, his piggy eyes hot. "Tole you and tole you she warn't no good. Now she's over yonder sayin' that my boy, Mike, here, and some of his friends raped her and them other whores with her. Said they made 'em take some dope. Why, my boy don't even drink much, Larry. She's lyin'. She . . ."

"Shut your goddamn mouth, Vic," I told him, stepping close. I looked over toward the smashed car and for an instant, my eyes caught a flash of raven hair and a very pale face, the forehead bandaged. She seemed so alone, so tiny, so vulnerable.

"Hey, Larry-boy!" Vic shouted. "You cain't talk to me like 'at. I'm your boss. I . . ."

"Vic?" I turned to face him, my face only inches from his. "Don't jack around with me. Not now, not ever. I'll tear your head off and piss down your neck. Your 'good boy' is a goddamn dope dealer. He's been selling dope to kids for years. The whole town knows it and so do the cops. Your son is a no-good, two-faced sorry-assed punk. And what he is, you helped make him. He and his friends gang-banged those girls. Now you may have enough stroke to buy him out of it. He may never go to trial or to prison for what he and his friends did . . ." The sky was beginning to lighten in the east, the first rays of silver pushing the darkness aside. ". . . But he's got me to answer to. And I'll get around to him. Eventually. And you, too, if you get in my way. So for now, you lard-assed tub of guts, just shut that flapping trap of yours. Keep it closed and don't bother me."

I pushed past him, leaving him with his mouth hanging open and his crappy kid hollering that what I said was all a bunch of lies. Vic finally found his voice and started yelling that I was fired. Get all my shit out of the office, get my clothes and stuff out of his company house, turn in my company car, and don't ever come back. Yeah.

"You can use my car until you can rent or buy one, Mr. Baldwin," my secretary, Jesse, called. She was with a group of other Goodman employees, all of them in various stages of dress, some in bathrobes.

"You're fired, too!" Vic yelled at her.

"Fuck you, fatso!" Jesse called.

I ignored Vic's rantings and walked over to Chief Pardue. He stepped back, a wary look in his eyes.

"How badly is she hurt, Chief?"

"I don't rightly know. She's banged up pretty bad. Simmons here was the first one on the scene."

I looked at Simmons, the cop who had once beaten Cody

and then taken advantage of her while she was unconscious. He would not meet my eyes. I watched a slow flush creep up his neck, covering his entire face, all the way to his hairline. "It's all going to come out, Simmons. And you know what I'm talking about." I glanced over at the car. It was still surrounded by EMTs and cops.

"I didn't do nothing'," Simmons muttered.

"You're a liar. But I'll get around to you." I cut my eyes to the chief. "Do yourself and me a big favor, Chief. Tell those people to let me speak to Cody."

He met my gaze. "I don't take orders from you, Baldwin."

"No. You don't. You take orders from Victor Goodman. That little brown spot on your nose comes from Vic's ass." I smiled at him. Very unpleasantly. I spoke softly but plainly. "I don't have many friends, Pardue. But the ones I have are in sensitive places. Like this buddy of mine on *The New York Times* and a cousin with *The Washington Post*." I was lying through my teeth. I knew absolutely no one on either paper, and the last I heard of any cousins of mine, one was in prison and the other a drunk. But lying was something I was good at—back then. "I think they'd both be very interested in this story. About how Simmons here got way out of line once with that young lady pinned in that wreckage after he beat and kicked her unconscious. After he stopped her, illegally, with no probable cause except the word of a dope dealer you and your people know about and protect because his father owns all of you. Want me to call those people, Pardue? Have them come in here and do some snooping? Maybe I could call another friend of mine with the Justice Department."

"Ah . . ." Pardue shook his head.

The chief had to be one stupid son of a bitch. He bought every word.

"Let Mr. Baldwin through, boys!" Pardue called. "Let him talk to the girl."

"Pardue!" Vic squalled. "What the hell do you think you're doin'?"

"Shut up, Mr. Goodman!" Pardue called. "For God's sake, just shut up. Don't make things no worser than they are."

"Don't you ever tell me to shut up, you redneck cracker!" Vic hollered. "I put you behind that badge and I can take it away any time."

Several hundred people were standing silently, listening to every word.

The EMTs and the cops backed off and let me through. I knelt beside Cody.

Her face was bloody and she was in great pain, sweat mingling with the blood. She tried a smile. "Hi, Larry. I was wondering when you'd get here," she whispered.

I put my hand gently on her shoulder. "They'll get you out of there, Cody. Just hang on."

Blood was leaking out of one corner of her mouth and I wondered how bad the internal injuries were.

"I must look terrible, Larry."

"You're beautiful."

"I bet you say that to all the girls."

I smiled at her.

"Mike and Woody and Cal started following us around. I thought I'd lost them. Drove out here and parked my car in the middle of all this junk. But they found us. It was awful,

Larry. They raped us, over and over again. But it's our word against theirs, and you know how that'll turn out."

"Don't talk, Cody. Just . . ." Just what? I didn't know what to say.

"I hurt so bad, Larry. My legs are broken."

Far in the distance, I could hear sirens. "Troopers are coming with Jaws, Cody. They're going to cut you out of there."

"Peggy and Brenda . . . have you seen them?"

I shook my head. "No, baby, I didn't see them."

"I got away from Mike and ran to my car. I'm naked from the waist down, Larry. They tore my jeans all to pieces getting them off me. Mike . . . he started after me in that damn big truck of his. He rammed me, over and over again. I was so scared. I must have lost consciousness. When I came to, all these people were here."

Cody slumped forward and I thought she had passed out. Then she moaned and lifted her head, opening her eyes.

"The rescue team is almost here, honey."

"Don't let all these people see me naked, Larry."

"I won't, Cody. I promise."

"I worry about us, Larry," she murmured.

Us? What the hell was she talking about?

"I wanted it. I really did. Now I'm afraid it's too late."

"We've been all through that, Cody. Don't talk about it now."

"You don't understand."

She was right about that.

The sirens were closer. I was scared. Not scared of losing her—I'd already done that. I'd screwed up her life royally.

The hell with mine. I would gladly have traded places with her in that twisted wreckage.

"I just know I have," she whispered. "I can feel it."

"Know you have what? Feel what? Can you wriggle your toes, Cody?"

"Oh, Larry. I'm not talking about me."

She was babbling. Delirious.

"I wonder if I'll ever get to see the valley of the butterflies," she said softly.

"Sure you will, Cody. After you get better."

"I hope so. I bet it's beautiful."

"You better step back now, Mr. Baldwin," one of the EMTs said.

I ignored him.

"I wanted it to be a little girl," Cody murmured.

She was pregnant. That was what she was talking about. That would account for the mood swings and the crying at work. Had to be. Pregnant. Why hadn't she told me?

"Mr. Baldwin," the EMT said. "Get out of the way, sir. She's losing consciousness. Move!"

"I'm going to see the butterflies," Cody whispered. "They're so lovely. Millions and millions of them." Her eyes closed and her head slumped forward.

"Get out of the damn way!" an EMT said, dropping a hand on my shoulder.

I stood up and stepped back and the EMTs moved in just as the rescue team roared up and jumped out and began gathering up all their equipment.

The Jaws were cranked up and for several minutes, the

early morning air was filled with the harsh sounds of metal being cut.

"Hurry up, goddammit!" an EMT shouted. "We're losing her."

"Dear God," I whispered.

The wreckage was cut away and Cody was taken from the smashed car and covered with a white sheet. Her blood quickly stained the sheet.

As she was pulled from the car, a small tennis shoe slipped from one foot. I picked it up. I remember the shoe was worn, with a hole beginning in the sole.

Cody never did have much money to spare.

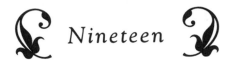

Nineteen

It took a whole passel of good ol' boys to pull me away from Cody, pin me to the ground, and sit on me while she was being loaded into the ambulance. Chief Pardue kept jumping around, hollering, "Don't hit him, boys! For God's sake, don't hit him."

When Cody was in the ambulance and it was moaning away, I relaxed and the citizens and cops let me up. They were wary—I had gotten in some pretty good licks before I was overwhelmed.

"Sorry, boys," I said. "Is she still alive?"

"Yes," a deputy said. "Are you all right now, Mr. Baldwin?"

No. And I never would be. "Yes," I said aloud. I didn't recognize my own voice.

The cops moved away from me. I think they were glad to go.

"She ain't got a chance," I heard one man say before his buddy could shush him up. "She's hurt real bad."

Another man said, "Let's get a rope and hang that goddamn Mike Goodman."

They wouldn't; but I thought that was a real good idea at the time. Still do.

The sirens faded just as the sun rose over the eastern horizon. I walked over to the company car—Benson was waiting for me.

"I been waiting for you, Mr. Baldwin. I'll have a car sent over to your house within the hour. Use it as long as you like. No charge."

I thanked him and he shook my hand.

At the company-owned house, I packed up my gear and when I was through, stowed it in back of the car Benson had been so kind as to let me use. Then I called Tom Vanderwedge for information. I didn't know where Cody had been taken or even if she was still alive.

"She was Medi-Vac'ed to Atlanta. Doctor Averett went with her. I just spoke with him. It isn't good, but she's going to make it. Internal injuries, both legs and her hip broken, one wrist and several ribs broken. Do you really love the girl, Baldwin?"

"More than I could ever say, Tom. Yes. I do love her."

"I think you're a fourteen-karat bastard, but somehow I feel sorry for you. I suppose God will forgive me for that."

"What hospital was she taken to?"

He told me. "They're pulling in the best people available, Larry."

"How long will she be under the knife?"

"I asked the doctor the same question. He said several hours. And there will probably be a number of operations."

"Will you call me, Tom? I'll be at the country house. You have the number."

"Yeah, you sorry son of a bitch. I'll call." He hung up. I didn't blame him for being angry. How could I? Everything he said was true.

I got to the country house about mid-morning. The house seemed full of her. I made a pot of coffee. Then, prowling around, I found a torn shirt and an old scarf of hers. I sat holding the shirt and scarf, sitting in My Chair, looking at Her Chair. It was the first time I'd been to the little house in quite a while. I sat, waiting for news. If I knew any prayers, I said them. I just don't remember.

Several hours dragged by, the longest hours of my life. Finally, Tom called. "She's going to be all right, Larry. Looks real good . . ."

I sighed and sat down in relief.

". . . There will be further surgery required, but right now, it's all right."

"Tom, how about those other girls?"

"They were raped for sure. I have a friend who works at the hospital. They're not going to press charges. Vic Goodman's been busy—he got to their parents and bought them off. But I don't know what he's going to do about Cody. I'm starting a fund to raise money for all this surgery. Cody doesn't have any hospitalization."

I thought of Vic. "Yes, she does, Tom."

"Oh?"

"Yeah. A real good policy. No limits. It provides for everything."

"I didn't know that."

"Tom, did Cody suffer any brain damage?"

"No. The doctors don't think so. Tell me more about this policy of Cody's."

"I'll get back to you about that, Tom."

"Do that." He hung up.

I stood by the phone for a few moments, then went into the bedroom and opened a trunk full of winter things and took out a pair of unlined leather gloves and put them in my pocket. I locked up the house and drove back into town.

I drove straight to Victor Goodman's sprawling mansion. I didn't knock, just pushed open the door with gloved hands and found Vic and his punk-ass son standing in the den.

"What the hell do you want, Baldwin?" Vic hollered.

I didn't say a word. I stepped in close and decked Vic first, catching him off guard and knocking him sprawling on his big, fat butt. Then I went after his slimy kid.

The punk thought he was bad, thought he was tough. After about sixty seconds he was screaming and begging. I don't really know how long I hammered on him. I quit when my fist started making splatting, smushing sounds as it hit his ruined face. His nose was gone. Blood spattered the expensive carpet. His teeth were all over the place and I had kicked his balls up into his belly. One ear was hanging by a single sliver of skin and the other one was swollen three times normal size. When I finally dropped him unconscious to the floor, Vic was on his hands and knees, holding his busted, bleeding mouth, and what would turn out to be a broken jaw. A plastic surgeon could rebuild his goddamn kid's face, but it would take many operations and a whole new set of teeth. The store-bought kind.

"Oh, God, Larry!" Vic moaned and mumbled. "He was

such a handsome boy. Just look at what you've gone and done to him."

I hauled Vic to his feet and gave him one-two in the belly and watched him huddle up into an obscene ball on the blood-splattered carpet. After I'd knocked Vic down twice and he wisely decided to stay down, he muttered that he "shore was glad his old lady wasn't here to see none of this."

She had gone to a bridge party. Her son is responsible for stalking and raping three young women, then almost killing Cody, and she goes off to a damn card party. This family deserved each other.

I threw Vic on a couch near a telephone. I balled my right hand into a fist and he cringed. "Don't hit me no more, Larry. Please!"

"I'm only going to say this one time, Vic, so you damn well better listen hard and get it straight. You ready? Good. Now then, you are going to call a hospital in Atlanta. I'll dial the number. You will speak to the hospital administrator and the chief of medicine and the finance office. Cody West gets the finest treatment available, Vic, anywhere in the world. Money is no object, because you're picking up the tab for everything. I can't do anything for those other girls your sorry-assed son and his equally sorry-assed punk friends raped—you've already bought off their parents. But you *will* help Cody. If she needs it, she will see the finest psychiatrists in the country. The best therapist. And if it takes five months, five years, or a lifetime to get her well, there'll be five hundred dollars deposited in her account. Every week. By you. And you are not going to miss a week. Ever. You own the local bank, Vic. For now. But by the time Cody's lawyers get through slicing up your fat ass, she might well own that bank, this house, the Goodman Company, and have you mopping floors."

I dialed the hospital and handed the phone to a terrified Victor Goodman. He was so scared I hoped he wouldn't have a heart attack and die on me before he could set things up. I poured him a glass of water and the bastard actually thanked me.

Vic got on the horn. With his power, he cut right through any red tape. He was very anxious to please me. He was so anxious there was a wet stain at his crotch. After he talked to the people at the hospital, he called his bank, then he called his lawyers, and at my instructions, he called Tom Vander- wedge. I told Tom to tape-record the conversation and he did, with Vic's understanding and authorization to do so. Vic's speech was slightly slurred—he'd found an old set of dentures to replace, temporarily, the ones I'd knocked out— but everybody would know it was good ol' Victor Goodman talking.

Then I had him call an Atlanta newspaper and speak to the day editor. He told him what he was doing. In detail. What a story! Yes, sir, Mr. Goodman, you are truly a great humanitarian. What a guy! I had Vic give the editor the names of the lawyers to contact for verification.

Tom Vanderwedge came over and nearly got sick at all the blood splattered around the den. Mike was still unconscious. Tom recovered nicely and shoved a legal document under Vic's nose and told him to sign it. Vic didn't hesitate a sec- ond. He was exhausted and in pain, but I was not quite through with him.

I leaned over Vic and said, "You listen to me, lard-ass. If you try to renege on any part of this deal, I'll know it. And I'll be back. I give you my personal promise that you will die a slow, miserable death."

"I don't want to hear any of this," Tom said, and beat it out the door.

I told Vic where I would start skinning him alive. I told him in great detail. He believed me, his face getting paler. He finally blurted, "Oh, my God!" Then he fainted, hitting the floor like a beached whale.

I called the local ambulance service and told them there had been an accident at the Goodman mansion—they'd better hurry right over. Father and son had gotten into an argument and then gone after each other. Then I warned them to keep the incident quiet, real quiet.

They assured me they would.

I left father and son unconscious on the floor and walked out into a soft Georgia rain. I did not know it had begun raining. Maybe the angels were crying. The raindrops felt good on my face. My right hand was swollen and there was a brittle, metallic, very bad taste in my mouth. But it was tempered with no small degree of satisfaction.

I drove over and cleaned out my office. I wrote a short letter of resignation and left it on Vic's desk. Then I went back to the little country house to wait for news about Cody.

The house seemed so silent. So empty. I could almost hear it sighing. It actually seemed to miss Cody as much as I did.

Almost.

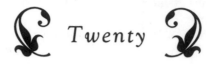

Twenty

The chief of psychiatry still didn't much care for me—I could read that in his eyes. But that was okay, for I didn't care all that much for me, either.

Cody had really taken a jolt, mentally, and the shrinks had their work cut out for them. Tom Vanderwedge had told the doctors what he knew about Cody and me, and the head shrink had called me, asking if I would talk with him. I told him I would do anything to help Cody. This was to be the last of what had turned out to be many meetings.

It was late fall in Georgia, the leaves changing colors and the temperature beginning to turn chilly as the sun went down. Soon I would be leaving. I doubted I would ever return. There were too many memories connected with this part of the country, too many things that would remind me of Cody.

I had spent a good part of the summer traveling. When I was in the area, I stayed out at the country house. I had bought the controlling interest in a very large and soon to be highly profitable company in the Midwest. But it didn't produce that kicky feeling in me that I thought it would. I had lost something along the way, but had also gained something. I wondered if they would eventually balance each other out.

I had told Tom that when I left, he should sell the country house and give the money to Cody—feed it in gradually with the money Vic was so graciously giving her, which was going to be for as long as she lived.

To my surprise, Vic had not contested anything. Not after the lawyers, his and mine, talked at length with him, and after they got a signed confession from Mike. Cody was now a moderately wealthy young lady. Once the town learned the whole dirty story, they were on her side one hundred and ten percent. Vic's power and his stranglehold on the county was broken. He had announced his retirement, effective the end of the year, and he and his wife were moving to Florida.

Chief Pardue retired, after firing all the cops under him, and the state police had, for a time, taken over law enforcement in Pine Hills until new personnel could be found and trained.

Pine Hills would finally become a very nice place in which to live and work.

Vic's punk kid was still undergoing surgery. I had been told that one more operation and his looks would be back. But I was also told that he was a very changed young man. He jumped at noises, sweated a lot, and had begun wetting the bed. I hoped he drowned in it.

The two other girls who were raped along with Cody had refused to speak of it; Vic's money had closed that chapter. Cal and Woody had been hauled in by state authorities and grilled—several times. A deputy sheriff told me that he suspected Cal and Woody would walk the straight and narrow for the rest of their lives.

"May I just have one last look at Cody?" I asked the shrink for about the hundredth time. "Not to talk to her, just to see her one more time?"

"No, Mr. Baldwin. You may not. And even if I did allow it, she wouldn't come rushing into your arms."

"That's the last thing I'd expect, Doctor," I replied as drily as possible. I could be just as shitty as this baldheaded shrink. Probably more so. I'd had a lot more practice.

He sighed and drummed his fingertips on the desk. "Mr. Baldwin, I don't believe you fully understand what I mean. Miss West . . . ah, well . . ."

"She doesn't want to see me," I said flatly. "Yes, Doctor, I understand that."

"Then why would you want to see her?"

"Well, goddammit!" I yelled as my temper flared, "maybe that's just none of your business."

He smiled. By God, he was human, after all. He sure had me fooled for weeks. "Forgive me, Mr. Baldwin. I only have Miss West's best interest at heart. I had to be . . . ah . . . certain of your feelings. It's quite obvious to me that you care deeply for her. You knew she was pregnant?"

"I finally figured that out."

"She lost the baby."

"I heard."

"It was a girl."

I said nothing.

He studied me for a moment longer and then nodded.

"Very well. You should, Mr. Baldwin, learn to control your temper." Again, he smiled. Faintly. I suspect he was out of practice. "How is your hand?"

I had broken some bones in my right hand hammering on Vic's crappy kid. "It's fine. Healed nicely." I suspect the shrink knew why Vic was footing all of Cody's bills, and they ran into the hundreds of thousands. But he had never said anything about it.

"When are you leaving?"

"Today. I'm packed and ready to go. Cody is financially secure. She'll have enough money to go to school, pursue a career, whatever she wants to do. I'll pull out when I get one last look at her."

"You're a stubborn man."

"So I've been told."

He nodded again. "The drug Cody was forced to ingest the night of the assault did no damage to her brain. She was very lucky, for it was PCP. Angel dust. And that can be very, very dangerous. Devastating." His face hardened momentarily. "I'd be willing to openly support the death penalty for drug pushers. I'd like to see them killed."

"I tried," I said with a smile.

He matched my smile. "Yes. You certainly did that, sir. Victor Goodman wanted this hospital to handle his son's, ah, physical and mental problems. I told him it was my professional opinion that a frontal lobotomy would do the trick for Mike. He took his business elsewhere."

I chuckled at that. "Back to Cody. She'll be all right?"

"Yes. I'm one hundred percent certain of that." He stood

up and stuck out his hand. I shook it. He sighed, paused, then said, "If you took the elevator to the fourth floor and walked to the hall window on the west side, you could look down on the sun deck and see Miss West. It's a warm day. I even saw a butterfly at the window a few moments ago. Lovely creatures, butterflies."

"Yes. They are that."

He studied my face again. "Well, goodbye and good luck in your new venture, Mr. Baldwin."

I couldn't resist one more dig. "And stay away from young ladies, huh?"

He smiled and then laughed. "Well . . . I didn't say that, sir. Mr. Baldwin? Before you go . . . a question, if you don't mind. I'm curious. Had . . . things turned out differently, do you believe you and Miss West could have made a success of your, ah, relationship?"

I didn't have to think about my reply. God knows, I'd given it hundreds of hours of thought over the past months. "I don't know, Doctor. I just don't know. Maybe so. I sure would have liked the time to find out."

"Yes," he said softly, and I knew he had been touched by Cody's charm. It was contagious. "I imagine so. We've all grown . . . ah, quite fond of Cody here. She's so . . . ah . . ."

"Much like a butterfly," I finished it for him.

His smile was open and honest and real. "Yes. Yes! That's it exactly. A beautiful butterfly. You know, she had a watch shaped like a butterfly."

"*Had* a watch, Doctor?"

"Yes. A young girl was admitted who'd been in a terrible

accident. She so admired the watch that Cody gave it to her. I thought it was a very noble gesture."

"Yeah. It was." Cody's way of ending it forever. Now she wouldn't have to look at the watch and remember. For Cody, it was over. "Goodbye, Doctor. And thanks."

"Goodbye, Mr. Baldwin."

I took the elevator, walked to the end of the corridor, and looked down at the sun deck. My eyes searched and found Cody. It was the first time I'd seen her since the accident, months back.

She was so beautiful and I loved her so much my heart felt ready to burst. Carmen had been right: I was so glad I had found true love and that I'd been able to share it with Cody. And she with me.

I felt the money clip she had given me pressing against my thigh. And in my jacket pocket was the handkerchief she had left in the cafe in Atlanta. Not that long ago, really.

I watched her for a time, thinking how lucky she was to be alive. She would make it, and I was glad for her.

"Don't lose your values, Cody," I whispered, adding silently: Don't ever misplace your sense of fairness, your ideals, your feelings for the underdogs in this hard world.

Standing by the window, I was wondering, as I had for months, how long true love really lasts. I had convinced myself that it would fade and vanish in time. Of course, so will the pyramids, given enough time and wind and sand.

I stared at her too long. She sensed it and turned in the wheelchair, looking all around with those pale eyes I loved so much. I ducked back so she wouldn't see me as she cocked her head in that special way of hers, a lock of raven hair falling over one eye. Velvet chains grabbed my heart and squeezed.

I turned and walked from the window to the elevators and hit the "Down" button.

I felt like I was descending into hell.

 *After Cody*

I made it out of the hospital and cut across the grass to the parking area, my thoughts only of Cody. I hope you find happiness, Cody. God knows, you deserve it.

I paused by a hedge, my eyes catching a bit of color.

A butterfly.

Extending my arm gently so I wouldn't frighten it away, I watched as the butterfly landed on the back of my hand, ever so gently.

"Don't touch the wings, mister," a child's voice said.

The butterfly still resting on the back of my hand, I turned around. A small boy, maybe six or seven, stood with a lady, holding her hand. I nodded at the woman and she smiled.

The boy said, "If you touch the wings, mister, you get that soft velvet stuff on your fingers. Sometimes it's awful hard to get off, and besides, if you treat a butterfly rough, they can't fly anymore."

"Yes. I know," I told him, my voice husky with emotion.

"I promise I'll be careful." Very careful, from now on.

"He has this . . . thing about butterflies," the woman explained. "I suppose he'll get over it."

I shook my head. "Not if he's lucky."

She looked at me strangely and they walked away. I stood with the butterfly still resting gently on my hand. Looking up, I saw sunlight blazing off raven hair.

"See that young woman up there, butterfly?" I whispered. "That's Cody. And I love her so much. Will you fly up there? She'd like that. She needs you."

Me, I'm tough. I don't need anyone.

But the lie would no longer wash. I was human after all. I was no longer a majority of one. I was a man who found he does have emotions. A man who refused to listen to his heart until it was too late.

The butterfly fluttered off my hand and toward Cody. I lost sight of it in the sun. But if I were a betting man, I'd bet it flew straight to her.

Fighting back the moisture in my burning eyes, I walked to my car. I had not cried since early childhood. Years of dryness, emptiness, deception, and meaningless assignation. No love at all. Until it was too late.

In the car, I gripped the steering wheel until my fingers ached, fighting back the inevitable. Finally, I surrendered.

There weren't that many tears. No great blubbering or sobbing. Just a steady outpouring of all that I had lied and schemed to possess, finally won, and then lost.

I wiped my eyes and pointed the car toward the Interstate. I wasn't really alone—I had enough memories to last a lifetime.

Get that soft velvet stuff on your fingers, mister, and it's hard to get off.

"Yeah," I said aloud. "That's what I'm afraid of."